THE FATHERLESS

ALASTAR'S URBAN WAR BOOK ONE OF COVERT EXISTENCE

Braedan Lalor

Creative Conflict Book Publishing

British Columbia, Canada

Abandoned and dangerous, survival is the only tradition.

Alastar's eyes popped open and it was night. He was laying on the table — still. Had all of that been a hallucination? Sophia was back again and she was shaking his shoulders. When Alastar focused his eyes upon her, she smiled.

"I have water, and carbohydrates." She poured some sort of flavored liquid into Alastar's mouth. "You have two more days to go, I heard a Keeper say it. You can do this, Alastar Daivi." Her eyes were staring into him — so softly. "I better go before I get us shot."

Sophia kissed him lightly on the cheek and spirited soundlessly away.

Praise For The Fatherless

"Intriguing characters and engaging plot. Can't put it down — looking forward to the next book!"
—Shelley Stark

"Unpredictable and action packed— Very much look forward to reading the next book in the series."
—Rob Adams

"A fearsome first novel from a compelling new voice. Read it."
—Stephen Small

Three young souls are locked into a life and death struggle inside a bloodthirsty youth culture. Fire, wilderness, poisoned steel and catacombs. Get ready for Alastar's urban war.

Being born was easy. Being stolen from our mothers — tougher, but Alastar and Sophia had to focus on two things: accruing strength and survival.

Being different didn't help Sophia because extreme sensitivity isn't always a gift. It helped Alastar though because he had been born cold — like all of the best soldier class operatives.

Survival of the ruthless is the norm, but it's the will of the Legend that's the new rule. This book tips its hat to classics such Ender's Game but has been described as the Outsiders meets Hunger Games.

Embedded with lethal peers, treacherous allies, and facing daily dangers — Sophia still has hope. With so little in their favor can these young operatives find a way to fulfill their destinies — or will they lose themselves to the greater struggle?

GET YOUR FREE DOWNLOAD

Sign up for Braedan's Reader's Group and get a free copy of **Dystopia Now**— Um, did I mention that this book is **Free for people that click below?**

Click here to get started

Www.BraedanLalor.com.

Books by Braedan Lalor

Covert Existence Series:

TheFatherless
TheResilient
TheBreakable

Covert Existence Related:

DystopiaNow

Creative Conflict Book Publishing
British Columbia, Canada
http://www.BraedanLalor.com
Publisher's Note: This is a work of fiction. Names, characters, places, and incidents are a product of the author's imagination. Locales and public names are sometimes used for atmospheric purposes. Any resemblance to actual people, living or dead, or to businesses, companies, events, institutions, or locales is completely coincidental.

Cover Artist: Joan Lalor

Image Credits: Rony Michaud, Michal Jarmoluk , 38471 pexels, 35393 pixabay, textures.com
Book Layout © 2015 BookDesignTemplates.com

The Fatherless/ Braedan Lalor. -- 1st ed.
ISBN 978-1-775274339

Dedication:

To my mother Rose-Marie, an exceptional woman of her time who has had a hand in raising every child that she has ever met. It was her who after reading the first chapter of The Fatherless, made me realize the obvious — the story mattered, *because they are children.*

To my mother, her hugs are hard but her heart is soft.

Foreword

Welcome to these pages. I am sincerely grateful to everyone who takes the time to read the Covert Existence series. An ancestor of mine — James Fintan Lalor was a writer as well. He was also a reluctant revolutionary (Wikipedia suggests that this may have earned him an early death after a stint in her Majesty's prison). Well perhaps the O'Lalor (O Leathlobhair in the original Gaelic) clan is not done making trouble. Although the days of British colonialism are far behind, the times that we do live in are not without their subtle and sometimes not so subtle dangers.

The books of the Covert Existence series are fiction, but they are also more than mere make believe. While these books are shamelessly adventurous they are also deeply reflective of the world that the author sees, in all of its wonder and decay.

I have tried to summon from the earth characters that breath and speak, and laugh and scream in bigger than life scenes, which are as improbable as they are relatable. May it be towards a purpose though, lest my writings be mere fancy and no longer worth your time or mine. I strongly believe in the sanctity of entertainment and of purification through escape, but when one can also have insight, inspiration, and thought as well — why would we not engorge ourselves upon all of it? The latter things are just as urgently needed.

Look around, reader. We live in a fallen world, but by no means a hopeless one. It is my wish that these tales of intrigue and survival might become beacons of hope and roadmaps to redemption — as well as sober warnings of things that we all hope will never come to pass.

On a side note, don't blame me if a disproportionate number of the women are beautiful, my characters are exceedingly adept, the conflict uncanny, or if the villains are bleeding style.

That's just the way I care to see the world.

"A gem cannot be polished without friction, nor a man perfected without trials."
—Lucius Annaeus Seneca

"During war, the laws are silent."
—Quintus Tullius Cicero

"We've got the right to choose it
There ain't no way we'll lose it
This is our life, this is our song

We'll fight the powers that be just
Don't pick our destiny 'cause
You don't know us, you don't belong

Oh we're not gonna take it
No, we ain't gonna take it
Oh we're not gonna take it, anymore"
—Twisted Sister

CONTENTS

ONE

It might as well have been blood.

Every drop of water that dripped off the ends of their noses, took with it a little bit of life sustaining heat. Death by hypothermia was just one cold mountain rain away for kids that were eight years old and under.

They had taught him the reason for that. They said that it was because kids had a greater surface area in proportion to their body's mass, than adults did. In other words more skin than meat, which meant quicker cooling.

The way that they were all huddled and shivering, and the chill blue tinge of their skin, made Alastar think that these kids would soon find themselves in eternal sleep.

He would have been curious to stay there and watch. To see what would happen to them all if they stayed put, but because Alastar was also eight years old, and because he had no desire to die just yet, he needed to find shelter as well.

He could stay and watch for a little while though.

Alastar crouched on the far edge of their camp, if you could call it a camp, and he listened to all the quiet bickering. Josh looked over at him, and then separated himself from the group, to stand nearer to Alastar. Josh looked cold. His t-shirt and denims were drenched, and his lips looked more purple than blue. It was hard to judge colors at night though, even on a clear evening like this one, with the moon full and luminous.

"We need a fire." The boy named Charlie said. It was the same whiny voice that had been annoying his peers since Charlie had learned to talk.

Bartus scowled. "Shut up Charlie. Even if we had dry matches, a fire would bring the twelvers down on us like a swarm of bees on honey." The twelvers were the older kids, roughly twelve years old, not that any Station resident knew their ages with any certainty.

"Bartus you're stupid. Bees don't swarm on honey, they make honey." When Sid made the said it, everyone had a laugh at Bartus's expense. People tended to listen to Sid.

"You knew what I meant!" Bartus wasn't going to back down from his statement. "Either way we're dead if we start a fire.".

"I think we're dead no matter what we do." Charlie said. Some of the whine in Charlie's voice was diminished by his chattering teeth.

"I say we attack them and get this over with." Sid said. It was a bold thing to say, but a few kids grunted their agreement.

Bartus was astonished. "Are you serious? We'd be killed. They're older and smarter, and they've got guns. We've only got rocks and sticks and knives. They've already killed most of the eleveners, and a bunch of tenners, and niners. We've got nothing to fight them with."

"We do have one thing." The voice was small, and distinctively female. Its light tone wafted into the encampment from the shadow of a tree branch, where a tiny girl with black hair and olive skin, was crouched.

All twenty-one pairs of desperate eyes drifted towards her. Perhaps it was the tinge of hope that they heard in her young voice, or perhaps it was because she was one of the strange ones.

Either way, the girl had everyone's attention.

"Alright Sophia, we're pretty much FUBAR enough that we gotta listen to your stupid ideas. So come on and tell us what we got that the twelvers don't got." Sid's voice always held a cruel tone whenever he addressed the young girl.

There was a momentary pause, and the silence of the night was only broken by the dripping of the rain on the leaves. But Sophia's answer came. "We got Alastar." She said.

Whatever feelings each of those kids might have experienced when they heard Sophia's words, they expressed it only in muted stillness. All except for Sid.

After a flicker of consideration he spat on the ground, and then spewed out his opinion. "Alastar? He's an eighter just like us! He don't have no guns or nothing either. Besides, he ain't even here so forget about him tonight. You got me and you all are going to do whatever I say, and Alastar can go chew sap, cause he's got nothin."

Sid eyed the members of his group, daring anyone to offer dissent. His rant went unchallenged until Josh threw in his chips. "Yeah, he's got nothing but brains, and thinking, and know-how, but I'd follow him over you any day, Sid." Everyone looked over at Josh and they were surprised to see that Alastar was standing near him, back in the shadows of the trees.

Sophia stood up quickly and dashed from her darkened recess, moving to Alastar's side and leaning into him like a frightened house cat. Alastar studied her curiously for a moment before saying anything. "Don't know if you kids got the strength to win this." He said. "Most of you are looking half dead. But I got more than brains, know-how and, what else did you say, Josh – a will that craves retribution?" The eighter's were silent; Sid somehow was even more silent than the rest.

Alastar paused, kicking at the dirt with his boot as though he was bored. "Yup. I also got guns, shelter, and food." Alastar watched as several of the dripping kid's lips broke into hesitant smiles.

Charlie wasn't impressed though. "We're still gonna die, you idiots."

Sophia stood up suddenly. "No! He'll save us." She spoke louder this time, and her voice squeaked with defiance. But then when everyone looked at her, she shrunk back into Alastar's shadow.

"How's he gonna beat the twelvers?" The voice came from somebody in the back of the group. "They're vicious."

"He'll just think of something." Josh said, as though that constituted a plan.

The group members were still whispering their opinions when Yari came up with a question. "Sophia. How's this gonna go? Is any of us gonna live?"

Once again everyone's attention fell onto Sophia. She lifted up her eyes and seemed to be trying to swallow her fear. Her eyes welled up as she readied her voice though, and a tear slowly traced its way down her cheek. "All my life, from when I was only four years old, I made a decision. If I always do what Alastar says, I live. So far, it's kept me alive. Do what he tells you and you'll all live."

The whispers resumed throughout the group. It wasn't possible to tell what the children thought of Sophia's statement. They did seem to be trying to decide whether they should do what Alastar told them though.

It went on for a while. The group didn't stop their chatter until Alastar finally stopped it. "Wait a second everyone." The children silenced. "I'm not your leader and you don't got to do what I say. Pick a new leader, and I'll help you."

Nobody spoke or moved.

Sophia could tell that not a single one of them was willing to risk calling themselves Leader when Alastar was around. With Alastar refusing to be Leader, and then ordering them to pick a new leader, it had created a philosophical dilemma for the group.

The silence lasted until Josh came up with the solution. "Alright Alastar, you're not the leader, I am." Josh stuck his thumb at his own chest. "And I'm gonna do whatever you tell me."

"You better." Alastar said, with a look that was as threatening as any eight year old could have made it.

For some reason, Sid just snapped. Sophia watched as he rediscovered both his courage and his voice. "Hey you buncha idiots, don't you see that if Josh is Leader and he does everything Alastar says, then it's actually Alastar that's being the leader."

Alastar stopped and smiled at Sid. It was a smile that Sophia loved, but how many times had she seen that charming sparkle inspire cold obedience in these boys? For several heavy seconds, Alastar studied Sid. Despite his earlier confidence, the wet and muddy boy couldn't help shifting under Alastar's dark scrutiny.

"What do you want me to do?" Josh said to Alastar.

"Take three guys and knock him out for me." Alastar was pointing to Sid, who took several steps backwards.

In the end four guys stepped up, volunteering to help knock Sid out. *A good crew.* Alastar thought. *Very eager.*

"Okay eighters, let's get you warm and dry — you bunch a little squeaks!" Alastar turned around and led his tiny army into the bush.

TWO

From the outset of the exercise the eighter's chances had been slim, simply because of age and experience. But when the group failed to reach the weapon and supply caches before the twelvers, their chances for survival plummeted to practically nil. That was how they had ended up cold, starving and on the run.

It had been days.

For Alastar, it was different though. He seldom ran with the rest of his pack. He had managed to capture two sniper rifles, a telescope, a couple of pistols, ammunition, and some provisions. It was significant, but it was still nothing compared to what the twelvers would have.

Alastar's first goal was to get his team dry, so he led them to higher ground, into a dense thicket of huge spruce trees. The branches of these massive trees were heavy with needles, and hung so low that the branches touched the ground. Alastar walked up to one of the big trees, and then pushed his way inside to where the trunk was. The closer he got to the tree's center, the more the space opened up until it was essentially a small, round room.

The best thing about the room was that it was perfectly dry. The others began to push their way into the tree like cattle into a barn. Even before four or five of them had entered, Alastar had already created a small, smokeless blaze, which he started with the dry tinder that he had on him.

One of the kids commented. "They'll see the fire."

"Not through the spruce, it spreads the smoke out." Alastar said.

"They'll smell the smoke." Another kid said.

"No. We're downwind of them."

The boy's jaw went slack with respect. "You've scouted their camp?"

Alastar simply smiled and went on with his work.

Dawn broke and none of the eighters were dead yet. Well, except for

Sid maybe. Nobody could say how he might be doing. Alastar got Josh to rouse the troops and then explained the plan. "Okay, we're gonna do what they expect us to do. We're gonna run from them."

"That's the plan?" Pax said as he munched on some of Alastar's peanuts. "It's just what they'll want us to do."

"So?" Alastar said, waiting.

"So when do we go kill them?"

"We don't. We'll let them kill themselves."

Several voices erupted into a dispute. *Kill themselves? That's stupid! No it's not.*

A fistfight began, but when the first kid pulled a knife, Josh ordered two of the others to take him down. Ten minutes later, the group had reached a unanimous decision. All of them hated Alastar's plan. Alastar pushed his way out from the tree's shelter, leaving Josh to continue the argument. The mountain air was crisp and the sounds of birds were echoing in the trees.

Alone.

Alastar would always be alone.

He believed that he probably knew as much about being alone as any boy could. Alone always made him think. Many times on past deep wilderness operations, he had wondered who his father and mother were. What kind of people were they? Were they cold like him? Had they passed on the killer gene, or had he stumbled onto that all by himself?

Alastar sometimes wondered if having a mother would have made him happy. Not likely. What could a mother do? How could she help him gain power? She wouldn't, instead she would want to control him. Probably the first thing that a mother would do, would be to dominate her child, and then she would force him to do her work. For that reason at least, Alastar was glad that the Station had taken him from her.

The Station had taught him how to be strong, and that was a good thing to know. Alastar looked around at the empty forest. The wind was whispering gently through the branches of the trees, which hid the eighters from their enemies. But why did he hate being alone? Shouldn't being alone have felt better? Also, if he hated being alone so much, why was it that whenever Alastar tried being around other people, he quickly felt like leaving them again? And as long as he was asking himself every futile question that his mind could conceive of, why was it that his stomach hurt in the morning after he had been dreaming?

"Alastar?" The voice was Sophia's. She was just a few feet behind him.

"Come on Soph, lets go see if my snares got anything." Then Alastar set off into the bush. Sophia followed of course. He knew that she would, she always did. He glanced back after a few minutes of travelling, and smiled as he watched her fighting her way through the trees.

Her dark Spanish hair was tangled and littered with twigs. Sophia was light on her feet and athletic, but she was such a little thing. She swore that she was seven and a half years old but to look at her, she seemed more like a sixer. Somehow though, she had managed to get herself accepted as an eighter. She had only succeeded in doing that because of her superhuman drive. A drive to place herself within Alastar's group, no matter what. Sophia seemed to be viscerally compelled to be near him, and Alastar had long accepted that her quiet determination, was irresistible. Eventually, all the eighters had just resigned themselves to her presence. Sophia was an eighter because Alastar was an eighter, and that was that.

Sophia didn't ever bother Alastar. He really didn't understand her fully, but she never caused him any trouble. Also, he never felt like he had to withdraw himself when Sophia was along. In fact, it was the best of both worlds, because when Sophia was with Alastar, he still felt alone, but of course he was with someone. Alastar liked that.

Three out of Alastar's eleven wire snares had caught rabbits. Fat ones too. He would eat well that morning.

The two of them ate the rabbits in a wooded nook away from the others, so that their greedy little horde of allies wouldn't beg off any of their meat. It would have been even better if they'd had the time to cook the rabbits, but either way, it was nice to have meat for breakfast. When they were finished their meal, Alastar started a fire.

Once it was going, he carried a flaming branch down to the spruce tree where the eighters were. The argument had persisted. Josh was standing outside of the spruce shelter with his arms crossed, having given up trying to convince the others to mobilize.

Alastar walked past him, smiling when he saw the look of frustration that was on Josh's face. Josh's eyebrows lifted a bit as Alastar carried the burning branch into the heart of the spruce tree. It was far too dry inside the tree's branches for a flaming brand, so Josh began backing away from the tree.

Ten seconds later a sharp crackling was coming from inside the tree.

Alastar emerged with a backpack, two rifles and some other supplies. He tossed one rifle to Josh along with a box of shells. "Tell the troops we're moving out." Alastar started westward, with Sophia falling into step just behind him.

Josh looked back towards the spruce tree, wondering if what he saw was smoke or mist.

Behind Alastar, screaming eight year olds began scrambling out of the tree from all sides. And within seconds a dense gray column of smoke was rising to the heavens, effectively marking the eighter's position for all the world to notice. It looked a lot like the pillar of smoke that Moses would have followed across the desert. Only this time, it was a bad omen for those who were hunted.

Josh smiled.

"Okay troops! Let's run for our lives!"

The man had seen so much. So many years had passed. So many fathers, so many sons. So much suffering but none ever suffered quite so much as an orphaned child. The man shifted his weight and hinged his knee bent. It let out an arthritic pop as he watched the ragged line of eighters, pushing forward on the valley floor below his lookout. The children strained and pressed forward, no doubt taxing every ounce of the will that was in them, as they struggled to maintain the narrowing gap between themselves and the pursuing army of older boys.

The man longed to see all of these children returned to their mothers, so that they could live their lives far from this horrible and perverse place. Some of the man's peers justified the current situation in their minds. They did it with erroneous intellectual constructs that leaned heavily on what these children were, and how they were unique. Most of these kids had been born, already scarred. They were a flawed design of what a human should have been, but this place made them worse.

Although most of the children had been diagnosed and confirmed as clinical psychopaths, it did not mean that they would have chosen evil. But with the hostile realities of the Station, a psychopath would choose nothing else. Just like any child soldier, these children had been conscripted and indoctrinated against their choosing, and that was the true injustice.

Sadly, every man would live by his own choices and that judgment would be final, regardless of their beginnings.

"It's a mine field."

"A what? Are you saying that you led us into a bottleneck valley with cliffs on sides, no real cover, and a minefield in our way! Have you lost your damn mind?"

"Have you lost your balls?" Alastar yelled back at Pax. "Take the rifle and go with Josh. When I signal, drive them towards us. If you kill a few, they'll move for the cover of those trees."

"And where are you all going to be?" Pax said.

"On the other side of the mine field, drawing them towards us."

Pax was instantly more at ease with his assignment. He had a gun after all, and he would get to take a secure position while the all others would be defenseless and exposed. Pax grinned. "Hey Alastar, this may be a dumb question, but how do you plan to get across the minefield? I don't see no feathers."

"We'll step where the mines aren't." Alastar said.

Pax looked at him quietly for a moment, and then shrugged. "Alright, it's your life. I'm glad to go with Josh. It's been nice knowing ya." Pax turned quickly and left.

Alastar explained the plan to the rest of the group. They weren't quite as happy as Pax was with their roles in the coming engagement, mostly because they had to follow Alastar through the minefield. "Look guys, Josh and Pax are taking more risk than you are. Just step where I tell you and you'll be fine."

Of course, Charlie had to make a whiny comment. "But how are we supposed to trust that you can see the underground mines? That's the dumbest thing I've ever heard of."

"Your the dumbest thing I ever heard of Charlie. Shut your hole and let Alastar explain." Josh said.

"Not much to explain. I know where the mines are. I watched them laying the minefield for two days and a night when I was five years old. We'll just go around the mines."

The silence that followed seemed to echo; as everyone's unspoken doubts filled the air like a fog. Even Josh looked a little bit concerned.

Charlie of course was the first to speak. "You were five years old? And they did it at night?" His voice squeaked with fear.

"They had flashlights. I could see where they were working."

"There's no way. Even with flashlights I couldn't remember all of that, and for that many years? Especially as a fiver!" Charlie said.

"That's true Charlie, but you're so stupid you think that a *mine* field is a field that you own." Instead of debating the merits of his plan with Charlie, Alastar decided to trust in his age-mates never ending fascination with *you're so stupid* jokes. He had successfully shut up his opposition with them in the past, and so far nobody had caught on to why he was doing it. The ploy worked because once the *you're so stupid* jokes started, they could not be stopped.

"*... You're so stupid you think a mountain pass is something you try to catch... Yeah Charlie, you're so stupid that you think a drop zone is where your piss falls when it misses the toilet... No, Charlie's so stupid that he thinks Op is spelled A-W-P ... He's so stupid that when the leader calls out that he can hear a chopper, Charlie gets hungry for stir fry.*" The eighters fell into frenzied laughter at Charlie's expense and when Alastar finally called the group forward, they all followed without complaint. After all, most of these kids barely cared whether they lived or died as long as they were well entertained while doing it.

As they walked, Josh sidled up to him. "So um — Alastar. Good work there with the morons, but it's still a bit hard for me to trust your little kid memories with my life, even if you do always know a lot of stuff that others don't. You got any way to reassure me?"

"Yeah, you can watch me." Alastar said as he halted the group with a hand signal. He nodded to Josh with a cavalier grin and then trudged ahead. After fifty feet, he broke into a run. His path curved, and zigged and zagged several times until he arrived at the far side of the clearing next to the trees. Then he turned back to Josh. "Now you try." Alastar called out gleefully.

"No thanks." Josh said unenthusiastically. Alastar hopped back towards them with the same dance-like randomness as before and stood beside Josh. Josh kicked at the dirt absently. "Okay, so you remember where the mines are."

Alastar smiled.

He led the group across the minefield in parties of six. When Sophia crossed, she was glued to Alastar's side like a second skin. She cried absently off and on for the whole way. When Alastar asked her why she was crying, she said that there was death in that place. "We won't die." Alastar said but her dark eyes looked at him as though his comment was naive.

Not five minutes after the eighters had all made it past the minefield, the twelvers entered the clearing. They looked big to the younger kids, who were all huddled in the trees. They looked mean too, and not one of those eighters had any doubts that the twelvers were going to be ruthless.

The twelvers spread out into disciplined formations as they picked their way forward across the open ground. They would have chosen that formation to limit any chance of them all being taken out all at once, not that any of them would have believed that the eighters they had been pursuing, were even armed. As Alastar watched, the twelvers covered the terrain systematically, like insects on the hunt.

The kid that was on point had reached the place where the eighters had been waiting while Alastar ran across the minefield. He halted the group with a hand signal as he studied the ground. The tracks were telling him a story that needed some sort of an explanation. Why had the eighters stopped and clustered? Their tracks went ahead, but not in any sensible pattern as far as the point man would see it. Then the kid made his way forward and noticed that the tracks were turning almost randomly. The point man had moved forward almost sixty feet before he began to wonder if the eighters had left those tracks just to slow them down. Then he signaled to the group again.

Suddenly a small girl with long black hair broke from the trees and darted across a small clearing before disappearing again into the forest. The twelvers tensed like wolves on the hunt, having spotted their quarry. Even the point man was on edge. The look that they had seen in the girl's eyes had been pure terror, and it had awoken the twelver's blood lust. The boy's began to move forward.

A lonely shot echoed to the sky and a twelver slumped to his knees, and the boys beside the fallen twelver grew concerned. Almost immediately, one of the other boys got swatted in the back by a long bullet. The group crouched low to determine the direction of the sniper fire. A third shot struck a kid in the throat, immediately followed by another which missed it's target but still ended up piercing another twelver's thigh, knocking him to the grass with a muted gasp.

Their situation was clear, there were two snipers shooting from different positions. It was a bad situation for the twelvers to have gotten caught in. The leader called out, ordering the crew forward just before taking a bullet in his own throat and staggering backward.

Seeing their leader fall was enough to cause the twelvers to surge forward en masse, towards the cover of the trees. Within seconds of mounting their charge, their ranks were thrown into confusion by multiple close ranged explosions. The confusion was heightened even further by the distracting presence of blood, and flying body parts.

To the eighters that were hiding in the trees, the explosions sounded like a symphony, erupting in alternating bursts of silence and thunder. Gunfire sounded from the nearby trees and took out any twelve year olds who looked like they might make it clear of the minefield. Hunkered down and hidden in the grass, a young girl with hair like midnight, was crying."

THREE

It had been a hopeless situation for those twelvers, a guaranteed defeat that would surely add to the legend of Alastar Daivi. The old man wondered if this could be the one. He also wondered about what might happen if he truly was.

Alastar Daivi was the only Station resident who had ever taken a last name. It wasn't a family name that he used though, since each and every one of them had been stripped from their families shortly after their births. It was merely a second name, and his boldness in taking that name had become a thing of true envy.

It turned out that there was one practical reason that Alastar had taken a second name, as useless as it was in a place like this. Certainly, it made him stand out in the crowd, but that wasn't always a good thing in the place like the Station. The old man knew though, that Alastar had taken the second name because of the void that was within him. Alastar didn't know about the void's existence, but the old man had seen Alastar musing about the void's effects. It was the void that made this boy seem distant towards his peers, and it was the void that caused him to at times be contemplative, while at other times steeped in melancholy.

A year ago the young girl Sophia, had recognized the void that was there in him, and she had tried to fix it. Through some convoluted applications of childish logic, she thought that a second name would help. So she had given him the name Daivi. She had picked it from a book in the library, because it meant *Beloved*.

The old man smiled at her choice.

The legend of Alastar Daivi was growing now every month, which was why the old man had been coming out to see this boy for himself. The youth's exploits had also reached the ears of some of the Station's self important rulers. Notably Studor, the Commander in this foul place, as well as the ears of Studor's immediate supervisor, whom Studor would know only as a voice on the telephone.

The office was frigid, but Studor didn't mind.

"Yes, it was an unexpected victory." Studor's voice was cold, and vaguely reptilian. Whatever had been said to him on the other end of the phone, it made Studor's face melt into a scowl.

"Well sir, one of the boys knew about the land mine's presence. He had watched them being laid years ago and took care to memorize the minefield's layout. Most prudent really. It turned out that the intel was enough to turn the tide of the battle." Again, Studor was forced to listen as his superior screamed at him through the phone. He held the phone inches away from his ear as he listened.

"Alastar sir, Alastar Daivi."

More talking.

"But sir he really is one of our best. This lad could shape the future of our organization. It would be very – ah, wasteful to do as you propose." This time the talking went on longer. "I see, so the family member who's name will not be mentioned, was there that night? What would a family member, especially that family member be doing in the dead of night, watching land mines being laid?

"Well, it is very unlucky, I'll give you that, but sir it's hardly a major security breach as you've called it. He's just a boy. A boy who has absolutely no idea who he has seen. A boy who is not at all likely to lay his feet upon free soil any time soon, if ever. This boy is a risk taker, he is unlikely to even survive to see his graduation. The last thing on Alastar's mind would be the men that he might have seen some night when he was five years old. I implore you to consider the asset that this young man will certainly grow to become in future years. He is a boy of destiny, I can assure you."

The voice on the other end had finally calmed somewhat, and Studor relaxed into his chair as he listened. "Yes sir. I will make sure that the boy is suitably punished for his victory."

Studor put down the phone and considered the types of torment that he would inflict upon the young Alastar Daivi. As he imagined the possibilities, Studor leaned back into his chair and smiled.

The old man had seen so much.

So many years and so much suffering. Suffering upon sufferings. So much suffering but perhaps none of them had suffered like this orphaned child. Alone, and so lonely.

The boy lay strapped to a metal table in the hot sun. In every limb there were several long needle like slivers, plunged deep into the sensitive parts of his flesh. It was a gusty day and each time the wind blew, the boy would tense and grit his teeth as the long needles swayed at the wind's touch. These children were born scarred, incomplete, and worse. Whatever souls they had, were being progressively deranged by the rigors of their environment. There was only one thing that could be certain; that was that this child would suffer more in the years to come.

Someone approached. It was a person that the man remembered from his own youth. The old man watched as Station commander Studor, who was also past his prime, moved towards the boy to view his handiwork. He stood next to Alastar for a while, exchanged a few words with the youth and then drifted off.

The boy was so alone, but not really. The man looked deep into the shadows of the trees, where a small dark haired girl squatted, watching. Her anxiety was visible at a glance. She suffered this punishment nearly as much as the youth.

The boy wasn't truly alone.

Then the man's attention drifted back to the boy. There was so much suffering there. He was very close to losing consciousness. Perhaps the boy could find comfort in a dream.

CHAPTER CAELESTE

Interlude

I may look young to those who would chance to see me, a young man, strong and in my prime. To them I might look powerful and limitless, but they do not see that I spend my existence on my knees.

Watching.

Hoping.

I have fought blade upon talon in the darkened skies, as Hannibal's elephant army took Italy. Yet I stood passively by, when Hitler's blitzkrieg tore a hole through Poland.

Today I watch a boy, grimacing in pain, each time the wind blows. And I see his tormentor coming to him. He speaks a few words and then departs. I also see an old man watching from a far off cliff, through a long lens, and I know that the old man has seen little Sophia, silently crying as she crouches in the bushes, observing her patient vigil for the boy that is so important to her.

It is not that I don't ever wonder, but unlike so many others, my wondering does not erode my trust. So today I watch as I did in Poland, as evil advances its will.

The boy will live through this day, but the scars he might ever carry with him.

FOUR

Alastar grunted and tensed as pain lanced from his hand all the way up into his brain. The pain invaded him like smelling salts, burning him into alertness. Most people would probably be praying for release by now. They would be pleading desperately to some inactive deity to make the pain stop, but Alastar knew better. Studor was the only god there. He held sway over the fate of all Station residents, and was unmoved by pleading.

Instead of prayers, Alastar used the gift that fate had bestowed upon him. It was a gift that all Type AB Psychopaths shared, the ability to compartmentalize their pain. To place it in a corner of their minds and close the door, muting its ill effects upon their person. Sure, the pain was still there, but it made the suffering less intense.

Less intense. He had been taught that much of what a psychopath felt was in fact, less intense. That was their gift, the source of their strength. It gave Alastar the ability to lose himself in the unique rhythms of this torture, and exist mostly within his mind, in his memories, and perhaps his dreams.

Alastar's dreams took him to a different windy day in history, to a real occurrence that had only happened to him six months ago. There had been an old man there, an oracle probably, stooped and withered and more than a little bit insane.

When Alastar first noticed him, he had been walking through the Station as though he owned the place, babbling about rays of light and tongues of shadow. An armed detail followed him, not to restrain the man but seemingly, they were there to protect him.

One moment that man was striding forward purposefully and the next moment he stopped on a dime. Then he turned towards Alastar. The old was squinting straight into him, with wrinkled and weeping eyes shot red like a person crazed.

"Child of Destiny, I think." He said out loud before he slapped his hand over his own mouth. Then the old man held his mouth tightly closed, darting his reddened eyes all around. Perhaps he was looking for eavesdroppers, but there was nobody around to hear, just Alastar and the Keepers that were acting as the old man's bodyguards.

Once the man recovered trust in the obedience of his own tongue, he slowly allowed his hand to come away from his mouth. Then he bared his teeth in a disjointed smile, which he aimed right at Alastar as he tented his fingers in front of him. *Like some type of holy man*, Alastar thought to himself.

"Oh no, not Holy, just wholly. The boss, yes? And you would be?"

Alastar wasn't quick to respond. He chose to let the man wait for his response, as repeated gusts of wind were buffeting their sides and tossing their hair. When Alastar finally judged the time to be right, he spoke in little more than a whisper. "Alastar Daivi."

"Beloved you say? We shall see." The old man glanced back at the Keepers in his security detail. Then he said to Alastar. "These men should never know, these men would have to go." The old man frowned and addressed the senior Keeper in a voice deep with authority. "Soldier, draw your weapon."

"Yes sir." The senior Keeper quickly obeyed.

"Would you point it at your second's head?"

"Yes sir, gladly sir."

"Then do it now." There was a visible tension in the two other subordinate soldiers, but neither of them dared reach for their own guns or even protest. Any act of defiance would likely spell certain death for them. Alastar wondered what they might have been thinking. Their best chance to survive the situation was to hope that it was merely an exercise in loyalty, which it probably was.

It wasn't. "Two each to the head, if you please." The shots echoed throughout the Station in quick succession. They were perfectly executed; the heads exploded towards the driving wind and the two men fell dead before they could move a foot.

In an artistic spray, diffuse splatters of blood droplets jetted from their skulls at odd angles. Then those same droplets were lifted gently onto the wind, and freckled all three remaining observers. The blood had turned each of them into a speckled canvas, that was a brilliant and blossoming red.

After the sole remaining Keeper holstered his sidearm, his brain was the next to explode. The old man had discharged a small caliber pistol, which he had drawn from his coat. In contrast to the Keeper's expertly aimed shots, the holes that had passed through the guard's mind and body, demonstrated little more artistry than a common street thug.

That left only Alastar. Still alive, and planning on staying that way.

Before the old man could turn back towards him, Alastar had closed the distance and met the old man. Wrist to hand, they grappled, size against youth, until with a twist Alastar claimed the weapon.

He wasn't fool enough to use it though; this was clearly a man in authority. Instead, hoping just to live through the day, he disarmed the gun quickly and stripped it down into its component pieces before the man could speak any protest. Then Alastar held out the disassembled weapon to the old man, adding a sparkle of contrition in his eyes for good measure.

"Your gun sir?" Alastar offered, keeping the bullets of course, he let those slip discretely into his pockets.

The old man actually laughed. He howled and snorted, and the fat on his sides shook like a wave. "Keep it, Beloved. You shall be my new security detail."

When he heard that, Alastar quickly reassembled the gun. "Hopefully, I can serve you longer than your last security detail?"

"Indeed." The man said as he laughed again.

The gust of the wind caught up his laughter and carried it away. Away and away, beloved. The wind, the wind, the wind and pain like lances in his flesh. He opened his eyes to a touch. To the here and now, where Sophia's small hand rested against his cheek. He was still on the table, with needles biting into his nerves.

"It's a dream." Sophia said. "An important dream."

"Yesss." Alastar said, but he was already fading. The dream, an important dream. The wind was blowing...

Such as a dream. They had marched straight to Studor's office, barging in without even knocking. Commander Studor jumped to his feet and was preparing to lash out at whatever idiot might be audacious enough to interrupt him in his seat of power. But then Studor saw the old man, and the anger dispersed. The Commander merely smiled.

"Can I help you?" He said in a saccharine tone.

"I need this boy for a while. We'll be in the Burrow and I don't expect us to be disturbed."

Studor said nothing. He wanted to speak, but he didn't. Instead he swallowed.

"Say it." The old man barked.

Studor's smile remained unchanged. "The boy, he is — especially dangerous. I wouldn't recommend it." Studor's cold eyes scanned the length and breadth of Alastar. "And today a very bloody boy, it seems. Oh yes, I see that you've armed him, what a wonderful idea." Studor served up his obedience with a side of cynicism and an even subtler portion of condescension.

Watching it all play out, Alastar began to enjoy himself. With a sharp click, Alastar drew the slide of his gun, moving the bullet into the chamber. Then he smiled at Studor.

Again, Studor swallowed. He let his eyes burn holes into Alastar as his Adam's apple shifted under the steel cords of his neck.

Alastar had never seen Studor act like that before.

"Oh quit with the posturing, you killers are all the same. Studor, I'm taking this boy. Get me a truck and supplies." He grabbed a pen off of Studor's desk and wrote down several items, which Alastar couldn't see because the old man's fat body was in the way. "These ones." He said as he slid the annotated paper toward Studor.

Studor found his tongue. "Sir, if I may add, this is all very unusual."

But the old man was already looking out the window, he seemed barely aware of Studors's flimsy objections. "Yes it is, yes it is. Talk the talk and work the biz." The old man muttered, then his eyes focused once more on Studor. "This boy needs an advocate," The man said, "You know this already. You can sense it in that withered reptilian soul that you killer's so often tout as the source of your strength. You already know it so don't you forget it, no."

Alastar and the old man took their leave of Studor. Once outside, the man ordered. "Go, get cleaned up. Get new clothes, and don't tell anyone, or I might have to shoot someone else." The threat was clear. The old man held out his hand. "Now the gun, Beloved."

In a few smooth but rapid motions, Alastar emptied the gun of bullets, and handed the harmless metal back to the man. Then he ran.

He went to his barracks first, and grabbed necessary items, stuffing them into his pack. Then he ran to the shower building and was surprised to find both Pete the sneak and Hank the prank. It was a wonder that those two were still alive, because the list of people that they had offended was legendary. Like Abbott and Costello, they were always up to something. Today, that something was adding chicken bouillon, hard candy, and red Kool-Aid into the hot water tank of the boy's showers. So anyone who used the showers was going to end up dyed red, sticky, and smelling like chicken soup

They nodded to Alastar when he came in. "I thought you barred the door — Why didn't you bar the door?" Pete said to Hank.

"Because if we got caught, Studor would have us shot for barring the door. Barring the door violates rule 26 section three, which states 'No resident shall fortify any area of the Station premises with the explicit purpose of restricting access to residents and/or Station staff.' That's what Studor would hit us with if we did it."

Alastar had to ask. "So what do you get if he catches you tainting the water supply and painting the residents red?"

Pete the sneak answered. "Nothing too bad, maybe a week without food."

"And we'll have to clean out the hot water tank, but that's totally worth it." Hank added.

Alastar left them to their work, but he also decided that he was going to wash up in the sink, using cold water only.

After Alastar made his way back to rendezvous with the old man, a bouncy truck ride brought him to an area on Station grounds, that he had seldom been to before. Most of the training ops were held in other quadrants.

As it turned out, the place that the old man took him to was 'the Burrow,' which was little more than a very secretive hole in the ground. Beyond that, Alastar's memory got hazy. Why was that? He should have been able to remember the details. Alastar remembered the old man, and a few spotty occurrences, but really nothing of substance. All that he could recall clearly was eventually leaving the Burrow, another bouncy truck ride, and then being tossed onto the floor outside of Studor's office. He laid there until Studor himself grabbed Alastar up and pulled him into his office.

"What happened?" Studor demanded as he shook Alastar's shoulders, but Alastar could not tell him anything. Studor shook him some more. There was more shaking and more pain, and the wind. The wind whistling.

Whistling.

Alastar's eyes popped open and it was nighttime. He was laying on the table still. Had all of that been a hallucination? Sophia had come back to the now once again, and of course she was shaking his shoulders. When Alastar managed to focus his eyes on her, Sophia smiled.

"I have water, and carbohydrates." She poured some sort of flavored liquid into Alastar's mouth. "You have two more days to go, I heard a Keeper say it. You can do this, Alastar Daivi." Her eyes were looking at him softly. "I better go before I get us shot."

She kissed him lightly on the cheek and spirited soundlessly away.

Alone under the clear night sky, Alastar Daivi was left to wonder once again, what had happened in the Burrow?

C H A P T E R F I V E

FIVE

Report to command center immediately.

That had been the note that was tacked to Sophia's barracks door, after she had finally dragged her tired and stiff body from the troop transport truck, to the only home she knew. Alastar had been watching her when she found the note. As she read it, Sophia felt Alastar's presence close behind her, reading along with her. She liked it when he stood close.

"Best go see what it's about." Alastar said. "You want me to walk you there?"

Always. "Only if you're going that way." Sophia smiled at him; he was growing up so handsome.

"I'm not." Alastar said, then he turned and walked away.

Wait! Dammit, that wasn't what she had wanted. "Check in on me after I get there!" She called after him. That way at least he could walk her home.

Alastar stopped. She felt his eyes on her, wondering something. Then her boy shrugged. "Sure, Soph."

Sophia pushed open the door to her barracks. She shared the little wooden building with three other girls her age. They were all niners now, so they only had to have four to a room, and she was glad that the others weren't there yet. Her oracle pod-mates could be emotionally tiring, even for her. Sophia looked down at the squat trunk bolted to the floor near the end of her bed; it contained everything that she owned. That trunk was a nearly overwhelming temptation to her.

For a bit, she considered changing into dry clothes because the ones that she had on were wet and muddy, and there was also blood. The blood had gotten into her boot and it was making her toes sticky. It would only take a minute to wash her foot and to change, but she knew that the note had said, *immediately*. And if it actually meant immediately, then she had to report *immediately*; otherwise things would happen. Specifically, things that she didn't want to happen. Sophia shivered and pushed the images from her mind.

She threw her ops pack down onto her bed and turned towards the door. Then in an act of willpower, she told her feet to march. It wasn't fair; Sophia was so tired. She walked to the command center with tears running down her cheeks, and the sixers and the seveners that she passed eyed her like a carnival prize. The young killers walking through the rows were trying to be threatening but most of them were still too young, and too dumb to do anything more than pick their noses.

Sophia remembered herself at that age. She had been so small then, nowhere near as big as her age-mates. She had been idealistic too, still holding onto ridiculous fantasies. Like being released into the open world and somehow reuniting with her mother. That had been a good one. Now Sophia only hoped that she might survive to leave the Station on her graduation day, despite how unlikely that seemed. But she had another hope as well. Sophia hoped that if she survived, that she wouldn't be irreparably deranged by then, like some of the older oracles that Sophia had seen.

Sophia could feel a black cloud of despair beginning to squeeze in on her, so she purged her mind of all of the thoughts about her precarious future. So much had changed as she had grown to become a niner. Those changes mostly only happened after she made the hard decision to leave childhood behind, and focus on survival. Alastar had helped her. He told her to put away her dreams and her longings and to buck up, day after day. *Whatever you had to do, just do it,* he had said. So she did it, but not all her dreams had died. In fact Sophia still had a sea of hope for him.

Her boy.

The Command center was just like it was on any other day, with instructors and Keepers filing in and out in a steady stream. Some residents were going in and out as well, often by force and under Keeper escort. Sophia walked up to the front entrance and a giant Keeper stood in front of her, barring her way.

"What do you want?"

"I'm supposed to come here. I got a note." Sophia said.

"I don't know anything about it." The big man said. "Screw off."

Sophia was considering what she might say when a prim looking woman poked her head out of the door to the Command center, and pointed a threatening finger at Sophia. "What are you standing there for? Get in here, you're late."

Sophia flitted up the three steps at the entrance and darted past the

Keeper. The inside of the Command center seemed dark to her. Sure it was well lit, but the darkness was stifling. The woman led her down a series of hallways, her low heels setting the tempo, clicking efficiently as they went along.

Soon Sophia was funneled into a small room with chairs, and some other children mindlessly waiting for their assignments. Three of the other kids were crying silently and quaking with fear, others sat perfectly still, with cold hearts and vacant emotions. There was no chair for Sophia though, so she leaned against the wall, trying to give her exhausted legs a measure of rest. As she was standing there, she wiggled her blood encrusted toe's free of the sticky congealed glob, that her foot and her sock were coated in, hoping that the assignment wouldn't take too long.

"You can sit with me?" It was a bright voice, almost melodic in it's rhythm. Sophia turned towards the source and saw a girl, small like her with full blond hair and a pretty smile. The girl was scooted over and she was offering half of her chair to Sophia. Sophia's legs could not refuse.

The girl giggled as Sophia sat down beside her. She kicked her feet back and forth as they hung off the chair, not quite touching the ground. Sophia had never seen this girl before but she didn't seem to be a killer, so she decided that it would be polite to talk to her. "Thank you for the chair." Sophia said.

In response, the girl's smile tripled in size and she leaned over and gave Sophia a silent hug. As a matter of fact, after the initial squeeze the blond girl never really let go. Instead she sighed, and left her head resting against Sophia's shoulder. Normally Sophia wouldn't allow that, but the girl had an exceptionally good feel.

"Who are you?" Sophia asked.

The blond girl smiled at her. "Your best friend." She said. Then she put her head gently back onto Sophia's shoulder.

Not knowing what to make of it, Sophia lapsed back to her private thoughts. But after the week that she had been having she didn't like what she found there, so Sophia decided to continue the conversation with the new girl. "You shouldn't be my friend, it's dangerous." Sophia told her. "I'm not like other oracles. I run with killers."

The girl's big blue eyes sharpened into focus as she looked at Sophia from up close. "Oh my. Have they ever killed you?"

What? That didn't even make sense, but Sophia wasn't about to be impolite when this girl was being so nice. "They try sometimes, but they've never killed me."

The girl nodded, her blue eyes serious. "My name's Demsie. I'm not crazy."

"I believe you. I'm Sophia."

Demsie's smiled brightened and she hugged Sophia with everything that she had, rocking Sophia back and forth on the seat as she clutched her new friend's shoulders. "I think we'll both love and hate tonight." Demsie said.

Cold fear slipped into Sophia's core.

Demsie had been right. Studor's assistant, Brigitte, had assigned the girl's as each other's partners. That turned out to be a blessing but the assignment, not surprisingly, was an unpleasant one.

They were given a list of barracks to search, fiver's barracks. *These children are of age*, Brigitte had told them all. *They need to learn to grow up, today. Go into each barracks and ask these fivers to surrender any of the contraband items of childhood, that they might have in their possession. Then search their rooms thoroughly, and any that you catch trying to hide contraband materials will be dealt with proactively, without delay.*

Proactively. Sophia could imagine Brigitte's idea of proactive. The kid's last year that had been caught hiding toys, were pushed into a twenty-foot hole, one after another. There was water in the hole though, so they only broke bones if they landed on their age-mates. Those fivers had been sentenced to twenty-four hours down there, and luckily most made it out.

Sophia hated being a part of anything like this, but she had absolutely no choice in the matter. Refusing to do the assignment would be dangerous, and it wouldn't help the fivers at all.

"I have an idea." Demsie whispered into her ear. "Let's just not tell her about the fiver's who try to hide their toys."

"Okay." Sophia whispered back, but she wasn't quite sure why they were whispering, since Brigitte and the others were no longer anywhere near. Sophia and Demsie made their way through the rows and approached to the first barracks. It was an oracle barracks, and all the five year olds should have been inside resting.

"Can I kick open the door?" Demsie asked Sophia.

"Sure." Sophia said.

Unlatching the handle first so that Demsie didn't hurt her foot, Sophia stepped aside. Demsie dealt the door a sharp impact with the heel of her foot, and the wooden door flew open with a clatter. "All right you little squeaks!" Demsie screamed. "Front and center, now! By direct order of Commander Studor, all inhabitants of barracks seventy-three in Pod two, are hereby commanded to surrender any and all playthings, toys, pastimes, or amusement items. Withholding any of the above said articles from us, Commander Studor's official agents, will qualify you for grievous penalties as deemed appropriate by Station Command. Do you squeaks have any questions?"

Not surprisingly, the room was silent; its inhabitants were stunned. Then one little fiver girl sat up on her bed and raised her hand. "Yes." Demsie said, pointing. "Little redhead with the dreadlocks, you have a question?"

"What does *hereby* and *grievous* mean?" The redhead said.

"It means your childhood is over, you'll be sixers in a few months and you gotta give up all your toys if you want to live." Demsie said. That plainer language seemed to get all the little oracle's attention. Suddenly the room was a whir of activity, with fivers everywhere. A small pile of contraband was rapidly forming at Sophia and Demsie's feet. There was a skipping rope made out of detonation cord, a ball constructed out of gauze and medical tape, even a bicycle, which was just a wooden wheel cleverly attached to a stick. Sophia and Demsie piled the toys outside of the barracks for pick-up and burning, and then got ready to go back in, to search the building themselves.

Outside Sophia took a deep breath, even as Demsie's hand snaked into her own. They both knew what was going to happen next. The toys that they had just acquired were only the giveaways. They were the toys that always floated around barracks like these. The giveaways had little to no sentimental value, and no deep inner significance in the fiver's lives.

Their true treasures, the things that these children leaned on for strength, and used to make it through to the next day, they would still be hidden inside. And Sophia and Demsie had to take them. Demsie pushed open the barracks door slowly, with tears running down her cheeks. Sophia stood beside her, feeling nearly overcome with sympathy as she looked at the fear in the fiver's eyes. Several of them were already crying.

Sophia noticed the redheaded girl with the dreadlocks glance quickly at her trunk before riveting her eyes straight ahead, and looking at anything but the trunk. Though it pained her to do it, Sophia moved closer to the girl. She could see the fiver's panic. Again the girl glanced at the trunk and then quickly away. When Sophia flipped open the lid of the trunk, the fiver started to squeal.

"Where is it?" Sophia said as sternly as she could muster.

The little girl shook her head, defiantly tousling her mop of red hair, refusing to answer Sophia's direct question. Sophia rummaged through the girl's belongings, but she didn't find any contraband, which meant that the fiver had built a secret compartment. What fiver's didn't ever seem to learn though, was that there were only a few ways to conceal a compartment inside one of these trunks, and every niner in the Station knew each and every method.

Sophia found the compartment easily and pulled out a golden locket. She opened it up and saw a picture of a woman. She was portrayed in a black and white photo, with stern features and an efficient bun on the top of her head.

The redhead was sobbing openly by that point. "You can't take her, you can't."

"Why not?" Demsie said, not a trace of harshness in her voice.

Tears streamed out from the girl's red eyes. "Because it's all I have of my mother." Then she collapsed into a needy heap onto her bed.

Sophia looked at the photograph again. By the look of the image, it was most likely taken in the late eighteen hundreds. Maybe this woman was a mother, but she wasn't this girl's mother. Sophia snapped the locket shut and put it into her pocket. "You'll keep memories of her from here on out." She told the girl, who promptly covered herself with her blankets. The redhead's sobs increased in intensity till the bed was shaking like an epileptic seizure. Sophia was just short of crying herself, but she fought to keep control.

Girl by girl, Sophia and Demsie stripped the fivers of everything in their lives that had meaning. There was a stuffed doll, which was little more than a sock filled with feathers and tied at the end, it didn't even have any distinguishing features. The stuffed sock that had been torn from Sophia's hands and thrown onto the pyre when she was a fiver, had at least had eyes and a mouth drawn onto it with a marker. She could remember what that had felt like, and without Alastar she might have just given up. It was a common thing for kids to lose hope after that annual event. Every single year there was a significant increase in deaths for the months following the Fiver Toy Doff, as it was called.

Sophia and Demsie also found secret chalk for hopscotch, a paper doll, two girls with friendship bracelets, and another detonation cord tied into a loop for playing Cat's Cradle. The first barrack's was the hardest, but it turned out that Sophia and Demsie made a good team. They cleaned out all their assigned barracks with the efficiency of professional maids, leaving the children behind to each other's consolation. It felt deeply wounding for Sophia to have had to play a part in such a cruel ritual, but the alternative if they had done her job poorly, would end up being much much worse. Certainly, some of those children would die, and some would turn to the dark side, but the ones that made it through would become stronger. They would need to be stronger if they were going to survive to be niners.

From that point on the survivors would grow up quick. They would study harder, train harder, and they would fight to make sense of the things around them that were hard to understand. They would become soldiers, and by the time they were eight, all of their earlier illusions would just be distant memories.

Sophia and Demsie sat slumped in their chairs in the Command center. They had completed the Toy Doff for their assigned barracks early, by nineteen-hundred and Sophia was in desperate need of food, and then sleep. But circumstance hadn't been kind to them, not at all.

All the other residents had been released to their barracks, but Sophia and Demsie were still waiting. Sophia wondered if they had been forgotten, but there wasn't any way to contact Brigitte, and nobody else in the center would give them even a second of their time whenever they tried to talk to anyone. So the girls waited, abandoned in that holding room, afraid to leave for fear that they would receive disciplinary action if they did.

"We should leave." Sophia said, frustrated. Demsie said nothing. Her expression said that she knew Sophia was just venting though, they had no real intention of leaving. Demsie was smart. "What time do you think it is?" Sophia said.

"After twenty-two thirty, for sure." Demsie said.

Sophia groaned, she wanted food and rest so bad. She slid out of her chair and cracked the door. There was a voice coming from down the hall. *There are those that rule and those who serve. But the servants all foolishly believe that they are the masters of their own fates.* It was a deep male voice that was speaking. *It's a lie, of course. A very clever lie, conceived in generations past, and given credence by hundreds of years of societal tradition, and structures.* Then the man chuckled. *We all want to believe that we are free but very few have the courage, or the opportunity to truly live in it. So we simply embrace the lies, and then we serve. The masters have always known that it would be so.*

Sophia closed the door carefully and crept back to Demsie. "There's someone talking out there."

Demsie smiled at Sophia. "But we don't have to hear it. Not if we don't want to."

Sophia had no idea what Demsie was talking about. "I'll tell you what Dems, if a chicken strolled down that hallway right now I would tackle it and eat it alive." Sophia said.

First Demsie frowned, and then she laughed. "You're hungry! Want a bun?" She pulled a squished and beaten bun out of her pocket, and held it up for Sophia to see.

Sophia stared at it as though it were a work of art. "I desperately want it." Sophia said.

"It's a good thing I have it then." Demsie handed Sophia the bun. It tasted like heaven. Only five minutes after the bun had been consumed though, Sophia grew restless again. She crept to the door once more and eased it open a crack.

Child soldiers are nothing new; neither is espionage, assassination, propaganda, or indentured servitude. In fact the people of the world are all slaves, whether they know it or not. It is all inconsequential.

Another person that Sophia couldn't quite make out was replying to the man's comment. It went on for a while and then the deep voiced man whose voice carried, started up again. *Yes, but backroom politics are not as backroom as people think. As a matter of fact they are very much, front room. Hell, the really lucrative deals are done practically in the lobby, in the full view of all. But people don't want to see it, so they don't.*

They all silently crave intellectual subjugation. They ignore all the facts, tucking them away from their conscious thoughts because they couldn't bare the consequences, if it were all true. They tell themselves things like; 'I'm going to be happy, I'll get where I want to be and then I'll —' Insert meaningless activity here. Then they'll say; 'And once I accomplish —' Insert another meaningless activity there.

The men began to laugh heartily, but this time together. After the laughter wound down, Sophia heard the sound of steps; someone was changing positions inside the room down the hall.

Haven't they noticed that the newspapers are selective about their reporting? A man with a different voice started speaking, he was a little easier to hear. *How about the inconsistencies of their world leaders? Do those men seem even a little bit ethical to the public? And yet the nations still all choose to trust, blindly and willingly. It's like a woman about to get raped by a friend, telling herself that it's not what it seems.*

Then a man stepped out into the hall and saw Sophia staring out of the crack in the door. Instantly, he moved back into his room and out of sight. *There's someone there, a young girl.* The deep voice said.

Sophia closed the door and bolted back to her chair. Heavy feet clomped towards her down the hall. Then the door to their holding room exploded open and a withered man in a grey suit was glaring at them. Sophia had seen him before, he was an economics instructor, and the way he was looking at her, Sophia was too terrified to speak.

Demsie wasn't. "Brigitte left us here and we want to go to our barracks." Demsie said. "Can we go now?"

The instructor was clearly frustrated. "Brigitte's gone, long gone!"

"Can we go?" Dems said.

The instructor gritted his teeth, then he waved his arm in a wildly angry gesture. "Go! Go!"

Both girls broke for the door, fled down the hall and disappeared into the night.

SIX

Alastar had no idea how the fight had started. It didn't matter really. What did matter, as usual was survival.

Things had always been about survival in the Station. It wasn't a very poetic truth, but the laws were binding just the same. Survival was the goddess-deity that all residents worshiped. Station residents had to be willing to either bow low at her feet, seeking her approval, or rise up in violence dropping bodies on her altar. Station residents would take whatever path they had to, if survival might smile upon them and grant them success.

That particular day's problem had started out with some fairly typical unrest in the easternmost part of Pod two, but it had flared up unexpectedly and rapidly ended up spreading to the edge of Pod four. When that happened, all hell broke loose, and if you could believe the hearsay, Pod seven was already in flames.

Not helping the situation, the Station's security forces, the Keepers had begun subduing and executing Station residents at random. While it may have started as a police action, the unique temperaments of Station citizens had allowed it to become a purge. Everyone who had a beef against anyone, was taking the opportunity to express their pent up and suppressed anger. Judging by their actions, the Station Keepers were determined to stop it without any regard for the cost that they exacted in Station resident lives.

The worst affected Pods housed mostly the younger kids, up to Alastar's general age. So there was no shortage of skirmishes igniting between his pod-mates, and no shortage of suppressive activity by the Keepers in Alastar's region.

Marauding bands of older killers had also begun cropping up. They were using the unrest as a cover, so that they could engage in sport hunting of the younger residents. Alastar was guessing that the older killers were most likely from Pod five or Pod three, so they would have had to have travelled a long distance in order to join in the fun.

Luckily for everyone, the majority of the older residents had been smart enough to stay home. Alastar couldn't be sure, but he suspected that many of the older residents would have seen purges in the past, and decided that they would rather live than hunt. But Alastar's idiotic age-mates in Pod two weren't nearly as insightful. The more mayhem his age-mates witnessed, the more they reveled in it. In the last few hours, his peers had effectively stirred the flames of violence into an all-consuming blaze, and Alastar was able to observe the whole thing as one great psychology experiment.

Then Alastar saw Sophia and he called out to her, she shouldn't have be out, it was too dangerous. Then he noticed that Sophia was also with Demsie, an oracle who had recently been transferred in from another pod. Alastar was disappointed to see that. They would need help and having Demsie along could slow them down. Other than Sophia, oracles couldn't usually keep up.

A moment later, Alastar caught a glimpse of Josh, Pax and Yari as well. The three of them had been trailing the girls, but the oracles hadn't noticed.

Alastar left his position and walked towards them. The three killers stopped cold when they saw him. If psychopaths could feel guilt, which they couldn't, Alastar would have said they looked guilty. They had definitely been stalking Sophia, and that made Alastar angry. "Push off, all three of you."

Pax and Yari were gone before Alastar could inhale. Josh took time to offer a quick look of regret to his age-mate, before he followed the other two.

Sophia and Demsie rushed towards him. Sophia's eyes were watchful and ready the way they should have been, while Demsie held Sophia's hand loosely and flashed Alastar a big smile. "I've been looking forward to this all week." Demsie said, grinning.

"The riot?"

"No. The outing. It should be quite fun if we smile enough."

Insane. Sophia's associate was completely insane. These girls could easily end up dead on this *outing*. He had to get them away from the violence, but how? The outer reaches of the Station grounds were nearly endless, extending for hundreds of miles in either direction. If they could get out of Pod two, they might escape the carnage, but Alastar knew that the Keepers had formed a defensive perimeter, and they would be awaiting runners eagerly, with their fingers on their triggers.

Alastar weighed his options. If they could get to the northeast edge of the Pod, they would be within five miles of Scum Lake, which had the biggest stand of bulrushes the world had ever seen. That would be good enough cover. Their problem was, getting there.

He pulled the girls over to the wall of a nearby barracks. "Get down, and stay here." He told them. Then he did one of the dumbest things that he had ever done in his life. He ran across an empty yard, dodging and diving in case he was in someone's sights. Part way there, a couple of bullets whizzed past his head, sounding like supersonic insects. Alastar dove sideways and fell behind two dead bodies that were lucky to be available, perhaps they were waiting to be used for just such a purpose. He hoped that the bodies would be thick enough to stop the bullets. As it turned out, it didn't matter because some other kid was dumb enough to charge out of hiding and make a run as well, and he drew the gunman's fire. Alastar was able to recognize the shooter. It was a Keeper. He seemed alone, about hundred and fifty feet away.

When Alastar saw the Keeper, his first instinct was to engage the man to get his gun, but even as he was planning the attack in his mind, he knew that it was futile. Alastar would never be able to shoot his way to safety. Against all the Station's security forces, he would lose for sure. The Keeper definitely deserved to die for shooting at Alastar, but his miserable life would be secure for now. Only though, because all Station residents were forced to kneel before the goddess of survival.

So Alastar resumed plan A. Staying low, he gator crawled to the wall of a storage and supply building. The supply buildings were generally taller than the barracks, which would give Alastar a bird's eye view of the purge. The building Alastar chose was even better suited to his purposes than other supply buildings, since it was taller due to an old bell tower that had been unused for many years. Also, the building that Alastar chose would certainly have other goodies which him and the girls would make use of. Alastar climbed up the sidewall of the building like a spider, using no more than the grooves in the old stonework as footholds. He was glad enough to reach the second floor window without getting any bullets in his ass, so he definitely didn't pause for long before slipping inside.

It was incredibly dark once he was inside the storage building, so Alastar hung from the windowsill and waited for his eyes to adjust. As he hung there, he heard a stir of motion from the far side of the room.

He wasn't alone.

After a minute, Alastar's eyes had become adjusted enough to see that his feet were only inches away from some wooden crates that were stacked up high. He let go of the ledge and landed on the wooden surface with less than a scuffing sound.

Then he saw the others. Three of them. It was the Dark Kings, as they had started calling themselves not so long ago. They were all idiots. Idiots who had no idea how much trouble giving themselves names of that sort could cause them. Not that Alastar cared, they would learn or they would die. Proclaiming themselves kings was guaranteed to try survival's patience.

The three were Bartus, Noble, and Ramsey, each one dumber than the next, but formidable fighters. For some reason, despite their lumbering wits, these three had risen into positions of popularity amongst the residents in Pod two. They were even beginning to collect minions, which in a world populated by power hungry Alpha males, was a sure way to get the kings dead. Unfortunately for the three of them, Alastar believed they were currently living out their best years.

"Your majesties." Alastar called out to them from his shadowy loft.

"That you Alastar? What you doing up there?" It was Bartus.

"Same as you three I imagine." Alastar let the three of them ponder his meaning, a tall task for the kings, due to the meager capacity of their stunted brains. Alastar jumped down from the crates, crossed the floor to a certain shelf, and rummaged a box until he found what he was looking for, then he darted over to another box, and so on. Inside a minute he had everything that he wanted and a camouflaged duffle bag to carry it all in.

The Dark Kings were watching him dumbly. He was just about to climb the bell tower and take a peak at the warzone, when Noble spoke up. "Hey, he can't do that. We said we were claiming this building and everything that's in it."

Of all the stupid notions. Alastar just kept climbing, but he also thought he would give Noble something to think about in order to stall any actions that the dimwitted brute might have been considering. "Of course my Liege's. What I do now, I do in service to you." Alastar called down toward Noble.

Alastar reached the top of the tower; the space was as dark and cramped as the inside of Noble's brain. It was a simple thing to pry an old board off of a window, allowing Alastar a front row seat to the carnage.

Once Alastar saw it, he realized that the fighting had become fearsome. The Station's residents were being pushed progressively north by a line of guards, who were stepping over the bodies of fallen children as casually as stepping over logs. There were flames in the Southeast, creating a thick wall of smoke that blew black and deadly across the eastern edge of Pod two.

The scene looked like one of God's judgment. Alastar suspected that whatever was in that smoke, it was more than likely lethal in certain doses. If the wind shifted just a bit, this whole situation would get serious for everyone. Really serious, really quickly. Alastar kept his assessment of the situation conservative — They're all probably gonna die. Making it to safety with the girls would be a long shot. But Alastar had always appreciated a good long shot, and the beginnings of a strategy were already forming in his mind.

Alastar heard some banging around below him and he glanced down. Ramsay was starting to climb up towards him. Unfortunately, it wasn't very likely that Ramsay would just want to chat. As Alastar began climbing down the narrow chute, a bullet exploded from the wood underneath his hand leaving only pain and numbness where Alastar had once felt a handhold.

That bullet was admittedly unlucky for Alastar, but it proved to be even unluckier for Ramsay. As Alastar fell, he tried desperately to find purchase on the sides of the bell tower. The best he could do was slow himself down, but he wasn't able to stop himself. That was how Ramsay made a contribution. The king served his subject by graciously absorbing the kinetic energy of Alastar's free fall, before continuing the downward journey in Alastar's place.

Alastar clung to the wall with all three of his working limbs. He shook out his numb hand, and paused long enough to notice Ramsay's thick skull meet the cement floor of the supply building.

The king is mostly dead; long live the king.

Alastar was pleased enough with how it all worked out, because if anyone could survive that impact, perhaps it would have been thick skulled Ramsay.

Alastar leapt to a pile of stacked crates and was already across the room and onto the floor before Bartus and Noble could react.

Unfortunately, now that he had seen the extent of what was going on outside, he knew that simply running away from Bartus and Noble was not enough. He needed to continue his shopping spree so that he could grab just one more item. Alastar ran past a perfectly good exit towards a set of shelves that at one point had contained gas masks. Unfortunately, things had changed since Alastar had last visited this place. The shelf only held boxes of tent pegs, hundreds of them. How could the Station ever use that many tent pegs?

He grabbed a handful.

When he turned, Bartus and Noble were blocking his exit, with their knuckles white and their teeth bared. Bartus held a damn big wrench, and Noble clenched two sticks that used to be a single broom handle, now broken into jagged halves.

"Are you hunting vampires, Noble? I promise you, if you back off now, I won't bite."

The two advanced. Size, weaponry, and superior numbers gave the kings their confidence, but Alastar didn't plan on fighting fair. He scrambled up the side of the shelving like it was a ladder, and before the Kings could react; he began pushing anything and everything down onto their heads. The boys cried out at the initial impacts.

The Kings would have probably been quick to move away and seek cover if Alastar hadn't leapt off of the high shelf, dropping like a true vampire might, swooping into their midst. He had tent pegs in each hand, and because he cared about the artistry of his craft, he held two of them in each hand with them extending from between his knuckles.

"And here is my bite." Alastar said, as he feinted towards Noble's neck. It caused Noble to raise an arm in defense, a poor defense as it turned out, because Alastar was able to use the prongs that were in his other hand to pierce the brachial artery of Noble's elbow. The spray of blood made it clear to everyone that Noble was out of this fight.

"Apply pressure." Alastar informed him, in case he had forgotten. Noble nodded as he retreated, probably believing that the advice was sincerely meant to be helpful.

Bartus didn't make the same mistake as his ally though. He didn't attack. Instead he chose the olive branch of peace. In fact, Bartus simply smiled at Alastar and then gave him permission to take anything he wanted. Alastar decided to take Bartus up on his kind offer, and he was certain to thank the lout before exiting through the front door.

When Alastar got back to where he had stashed Sophia and Demsie, he became concerned that he might have taken too long. Perhaps the hostilities had swallowed the girls up because they didn't seem to be anywhere in sight.

"He's here." Alastar heard a whisper from behind.

He turned toward the sound and was surprised when an inconspicuous strip of tarp got pulled aside, revealing a small blond girl grinning ear to ear, and a Latina child who's onyx eyes were streaked wet with tears. "It was Sophia's idea. We made ourselves small." Demsie said cheerfully.

They really did. Alastar couldn't believe that they had both been under that tarp.

"Come on then, quickly." Low and fast, he led them south and then east. He was paying close attention to the wind's direction, and had little more than hope to ensure that the toxic gas wouldn't shift towards them. The three of them progressed forwards as a tight group. No bullets whizzed past them, and there were no Keepers blocking their path. Why would there have been anyone trying to stop them? After all, Alastar was leading the girls right into a massive smoking black cloud, of death.

The area that was burning housed two things that were best kept on the outskirts of any population. One was the Station's dumps, and the other was a chemical depot. Based on where he saw the flames, Alastar was optimistic that most of the dense smoke was from the burning of old tires, rather than from the combustion of complex chemical compounds that would melt the flesh off of their bones if it were to touch them. Either way, Alastar was eager to get this part of his plan over with. In ten or fifteen minutes, most of the chemical depot building would certainly be consumed, and the smoke blowing from that fire would become toxic enough to raise the dead.

Alastar reached into his duffle bags and pulled out the gas masks. "Put these on. Do it right or you're going to die." He told them.

"But I don't want to die." Demsie said. "Not at all."

"Me either." Sophia agreed. "Just do whatever he tells you and it'll be okay."

Alastar looked back at the girls. "Less chit-chat, more action." He said.

Demsie laughed at the word chit-chat. "I like this." She said.

The oracles put the masks on and fastened the buckles perfectly, as though they wore gas masks every day. "Alright hold hands and follow me." Alastar stepped into the smoke and aimed himself vaguely in the direction that he wanted to go. The slick black cloud reached out to embrace them and swirled around their bodies. It tingled on the exposed parts of his skin, but so far his flesh hadn't congealed or sloughed off. So for that at least, he was grateful.

After walking through the dark rolling soup for about a minute, Alastar came to realize how foolish his plan had been. Navigation was going to be pretty much impossible. With all the debris and bodies strewn in their path, and with each person in their small human chain pulling in a slightly different direction, Alastar realized that he had no way to reliably get them to where he wanted to go. The smoke had been a good idea in that they wouldn't encounter any living thing within it's darkness, but now he realized that there was a very good reason for that.

Discouragement rankled at his mood. He tried to navigate by the feel of the wind on his skin, but the smoke had coated him in a black film as inky as pitch, which impaired his sensation. All that Alastar could think to do was to press on.

They walked for several minutes, quickly. As time passed Alastar became eager to make it through the horrific maze of darkness so that he could deal with more familiar challenges, such as bullets and flames. As they staggered blindly forward, Alastar began believing that they had probably been in the smoke for too long. The chemical depot would have at least started burning by that time, which meant that almost anything could soon be released into that smoke.

Then Alastar felt a tug from behind. He stopped.

He had been holding Sophia's hand in his, but he felt another hand clawing up his arm, across his chest and then down to his other arm. It grasped his left hand. The hand had to be Demsie's.

The three of them stood, with each other's hands held in a small circle, and black death rolling past them. *Ashes, ashes, we all fall down*, Alastar thought grimly to himself. Then he felt Demsie's hand twitch, and then it twitched again.

Short squeezes and long squeezes, they were dots and dashes, it was Morse code. She wanted him to follow her. All right, why not let the blind lead the blind for not so big a change. Demsie pulled them along in a chain on a course further to the right of where Alastar would have taken them. Along the way, they encountered a building, a car, and a low fence that Demsie led them over, and then they wandered across a field with high grass. It was still too black to see.

Alastar liked that they had found high grass though; he hoped that it meant they were getting close to where Alastar had been trying to get them to in the first place.

It wasn't long before the smoke began to thin. After wiping off the lenses of his mask, Alastar could begin to see the dark outlines of the girl's, and later was able to see some details of the ground at his feet.

Then the high grasses just stopped and they were replaced by scorched black earth. The change in the terrain happened just as the smoke had begun to thin and Alastar felt that he could even make out some detail in the landscape, beyond the haze. In fact, he could see hills. That had to be the mortar range, which meant that the fence they had hopped over was the one meant to keep careless people from wandering out there.

Alastar gathered the girls into the same hand circle that Demsie used, and requested the lead back from Demsie. She danced happily for a few steps, probably because Alastar had asked her instead of just taking it. *Affirmative*, she coded.

Alastar had the three of them split up. They got low and crawled like lizards in the black dirt, just along the edges of the smoke. He hoped that between the smoky haze and the blackness of their bodies, they would look like nothing more than the dirt and the smoke that they were moving with.

Twice they saw sentries walking outside of the haze and once they heard a gunshot, followed by a young voice, wailing. Each time there was any sign of a Keeper, the three of them laid still and quiet, becoming the mud that the others walked on.

As they continued, their smoke cover got thinner and thinner. When Alastar deemed it safe, the three of them rose up again, and evolved from dirt, to lizards, and then to almost human within a fairly few steps. He looked at the oracles that were following him. They looked like aliens, a dark and deadly variety.

Soon the three of them entered a land of grasses again, but this time there were also low lying bushes. The air had become clear, so Alastar pulled off his mask. The girls did the same. Alastar squatted down and reached into his bag, pulling out two clean sets of sniper's concealment suits, and hats with netting. One set he tossed to Sophia. "Here put this on."

She caught it and stared at him with her incredibly dark eyes. He had to smile at her black face and lips, contracted with the white parts of her eyes and the deep black pools that made up her irises and her pupils. Sophia didn't smile back at him though. Instead she began stripping down to put on the sniper gear.

"What about me?" Demsie said, almost dejected.

"You ride in the drag bag." At that the girl smiled and nestled herself into Alastar's duffle.

Gathering branches and grasses from the immediate area, Alastar decorated himself, Demsie's bag, and Sophia, so that they would be largely invisible to the passing eye. Sophia was frowning the whole time. "It's okay." He whispered quietly to Sophia, but a silent tear ran down her cheek anyway. "We'll get through this."

Her eyes turned towards his. "You don't know the screaming." She said.

What did that mean?

Like snipers, they moved low and slow. The three of them slid along behind bushes, and through open fields, changing their foliage slightly as the land changed its decor. At one point Alastar saw two snipers resting on a hill. Cocky sons of bitches. They were allowing themselves to be seen in silhouette. Maybe they even had a right to be cocky. After all they did have the guns, and nobody else did. Alastar was determined to get past them though. He pulled the Demsie bag up onto his body so that he would have better control of its position. She giggled as he did so. "Quiet now, enemies close." He warned her.

Signaling for Sophia to keep her eyes on him, they began to make their way across the open field, right under the noses of the snipers. It took hours for them to reach the safety of the bulrushes on the far side of that field. He couldn't be sure, but he thought that Demsie might even have been asleep inside the bag. A couple of times, Alastar thought he could hear her breathing, deep and rhythmic.

Once they were well concealed by the high marsh plants, Alastar unzipped Demsie, and sat back to rest. Without saying anything, Sophia sat herself right in Alastar's lap and leaned her face onto his chest, then she shuddered. Demsie seemed in no hurry to wake up and Sophia seemed in no hurry to move, so they sat still, letting the girls rest for the time being. Soon sunset would be coming and they would make their way to a place that Alastar knew of. It would work well as a camp.

At what he felt was the right time, Alastar stirred the girls to movement. "Are you ready to go?" He said.

Sophia's eyes were red from crying. "People weren't meant for this, Alastar. How long till these things add up and steal —" Then Sophia choked up.

"We're alive," Alastar said. "It's okay now."

Sophia just looked at him; she looked tired. "You don't understand. You don't know the dangers."

Alastar had never heard anything more ridiculous. He had considered every danger, and they were all gonna be fine.

The reeds were perfect cover, especially in the blowing wind. No one would notice their passing, if they were careful. They traversed through the extensive wetlands and reached the shores of Scum Lake quickly. At the lake, the three of them cleaned off the filth as effectively as they could. Then they crept back into the high rushes and travelled parallel to the shore until they were far from the violence.

Alastar led his brave but exhausted oracles to a little camp, deep under the root of a massive fallen tree. He had camped there before, and everything was ready and waiting for them. This place would be safe.

When the sun set and the sky turned black, the three of them crept out from under the tree and towards the water, more out of preference than necessity. There they stripped off their soiled clothes and swam under the smallest sliver of the moon, no longer really caring anymore if anyone heard them. They splashed and laughed out loud as they played in that water, and Demsie declared that this was just as she had known it would be.

Morning came, and in adherence to Station tradition, all charges were forgiven for those that eluded capture until the dawn.

SEVEN

It had seemed long ago, the night that they had camped near the shore of Scum lake. It wasn't long before Station business was back in full swing once again. Repairs had been made, the bodies were buried in mass graves, and that was it.

The lessons of the purging would last only until the kids that were involved in the purge had grown up and graduated from the Station, or died of course. Which meant that someday, there would be a younger generation ripe with pride, that would once again rise up and test the resolve of their masters.

It all meant nothing to Alastar though. With the purge now just a memory, Alastar's focus had been set onto less lethal matters.

Language class that day was about Baltic accents. They were given a ten minute break before the next block, which was likely to involve impossible physical strains and extreme temperatures of some kind. After conditioning, they would be allowed to forage the woods for food, and then they wouldn't be expected back in the pods until an hour after nightfall.

A treat, which Alastar was looking forward to.

He wanted to log some time alone. Ever since the victory in the minefield all those years ago, the kids in his age group, recently turned tenners now, rarely gave him a second's rest. They all nodded to him as he walked past them as though he was their leader or something.

Alastar didn't want to be their leader, although he was fine with some of them being around. Sophia was okay, and her friend Demsie was fine, even though Demsie was completely out of her mind. She was also consistently pleasant, and usually quiet. Sophia seemed comforted by Demsie's presence, so that also made it a positive. Josh was alright to be around too, but wherever he went, it wouldn't be long before Pax and Yari arrived as well. The other inner circle followers that Alastar had somehow attracted, were Pete the sneak and Hank the prank. The two of them came as a package deal and they had been sharing their ideas for wreaking random havoc with Alastar, ever since he had caught them pranking the showers when they were all eighters. That was just before Alastar had been taken to the Burrow with the old man.

Who was he anyways, and why had everyone seemed deferent to him?

Alastar shook his head to clear it. The Burrow was a mystery best forgotten. It had nothing whatsoever to do with keeping him alive for yet another week, therefore it was completely irrelevant.

Alastar stopped suddenly and Sophia carelessly bumped into his back. Alastar had known that she was trailing him. She always was. Tousled black hair, quiet as a mouse and two steps behind, that was her. He turned to grin at her.

"Sorry." She said, then she looked across the yard. "Oh, there's Demsie." Most ten year olds would probably wave when they saw a friend, but not oracles, for them it was dangerous to draw attention to themselves with a wave.

Demsie knew she had been spotted though and she scurried over, weaving a careful path between the milling psychopaths.

"Hi Sophia." The girl said in a whisper. In acknowledgement, her eyes rolled momentarily up towards Alastar's but she wasn't daring to make any real eye contact.

"Hey Demsie." Alastar said.

"Don't scare her, Alastar." Sophia frowned at him.

"I can't help it, she's just afraid."

"I'm not scared of him." Demsie whispered. "I'm scared of them."

"What?" Alastar asked.

"Dead things." Demsie said. "They want to pull my voice out."

Alastar smiled. He kinda loved Demsie's unique form of crazy. "How do they get your voice? Do they latch on with suction cups, or do they use stainless steel forceps?"

Demsie studied Alastar carefully before replying. "That's crazy." The crazy girl said. "They'll just use their hands and the vacuum of space."

Alastar laughed, earning himself a sharp glare from Sophia. She put an arm around Demsie. "It's okay Demsie, he doesn't get you. Don't think about *them* anymore, okay? Now, where do you want me and Alastar to bring you after conditioning?"

Alastar was surprised to hear himself being volunteered for service. "Wait a minute Sophia, I'm not an orderly in an insane asylum, Demsie can go wherever she wants and takes her own chances as she does it. I want to be left alone."

Sophia turned big eyes upwards towards Alastar. "Suit yourself, I just thought you might want to make the smart play and get some intel on the Station's newest threat."

"Newest threat? What are you yakking about now, Soph?"

"Just more oracle crazy-talk." Sophia said, not bothering to hide her anger. "You don't need to trouble yourself, with insignificants like us."

"Come on Sophia, I don't think you're insignificant and you know that. Demsie's insignificant."

A silent tear rolled down Demsie's cheek. It demonstrated one of the two things that Alastar liked about Demsie, she was either completely quiet, or she was strangely entertaining. For some reason that moved him a little, the quietness not the tear. "Alright I'll take her somewhere, as long as you tell me about this supposed *new threat*. Where we going, Demsie?"

Demsie smiled as she reached for the sky, wonder filling her face. "It's so beautiful." Then she turned and pointed to a place halfway up a nearby mountain. "Over there. Take me to Middle Field, it's safe there and we can see down is falling." Then Alastar watched as Demsie's attention clouded over with the dense fog of delusions in which Demsie lived.

Alastar laughed at her again. There she was, being entertaining. He couldn't help himself from egging the little oracle on. "Demsie, you idiot, we don't need to see that down is falling, down is always falling, and up is flying."

The girl looked confused now. "Down is *always* falling? And why is up flying? — Oh, you mean, hmmm." Demsie paused momentarily before her eyes lit up with excitement and understanding. "No, I mean goose down, it's falling all around there, and fat geese too, which we can eat."

Fat geese? That did sound good. Much better than the usual thin gruel that they were typically fed, and infinitely better than the wild leaves and roots that Alastar had intended to eat today.

"Okay, sure. I'm up for a serving of crazy goose pie today. Let's go to Middle Field."

Demsie seemed glad about Alastar's willingness to go, but Sophia was still tugging at his sleeve. "We can't stay at Middle Field with Demsie. The threat, remember?" Sophia's dark eyebrows arched intently at Alastar.

"Okay. What's the new threat?"

"Check him out yourself. He's sneaky, skinny, and he has dark hair and a boring face. Walking east, you can get visual at your four o'clock in five, four, three, two, one."

Alastar spun quickly to his four o'clock direction and saw the kid Sophia was referring to. Based on the skinny kid's look of dumb shock, he had been actively watching their group. It was clear that the guy wasn't expecting to be I.D'ed.

"Good work, Soph." Alastar muttered as he set out toward the kid. He needed to find out why the new kid had been looking at them. The kid moved casually through the crowd of Station residents, and then suddenly, he was gone. Where did he go? Dammit this scrawny kid must have been half made of smoke. How could he have disappeared like that?

Alastar turned to head back toward Sophia and Demsie, and then it was his turn to be shocked. The skinny kid was there, cruising slowly past the girls, like a ghost. He even paused to run his hands ever so softly through Demsie's blonde hair. If she even noticed the contact, Demsie didn't let on, and then once again he was gone. He had melted out of sight like fog under the hot sun.

Alastar trotted back to the two oracles. "Did you see him? He was right here."

"Who?" Demsie said as her eyes darted. "Was it *Them*?" Then she took a deep breath and held it.

Sophia nudged her friend. "That won't work Demsie, if they want to rip out your voice you can't stop them. You'd just have to wait until your voice grows back." Then she turned to Alastar. "I know where to find him you know. The skinny boy." She added in case Alastar wasn't sure who they were talking about.

"Where?"

"I don't now where it is, but it's a place that's called the Burrow."

Alastar smiled grimly to himself. It was strange how he couldn't seem to leave that place behind.

The conditioning session that day had been brutal. Of course, it always was. It was more brutal for the Oracles though, who weren't ever able to take quite as much punishment as the rest of them. Alastar was a bit embarrassed for them about that, he even had to support Sophia and Demsie for the walk back to their barracks. The whole way, Demsie was whispering under her breath, something delusional no doubt.

He brought them into their barracks and threw them both onto the same bed. There they lay. "I can't feel my legs." Sophia said.

"I'm not rubbing them." Alastar said. "Tell me now if we're still going on your little expedition, Sophia, because I got things I wanna do."

Sophia's dark eyes focused on him, which clearly expressed her opinion of how she thought of Alastar's prodding.

"C'mon Sophia. Put on some dry clothes and move yer ass before I strip you both naked and make you hike bare butt."

At that Sophia smiled. "You're lying. You wouldn't."

"I would and I will." Alastar's expression was stern.

Then Sophia laughed and pulled herself into a sitting position. "Okay, we'll be out in five minutes. You go and get your own clothes dry, you liar."

Alastar smiled once his back was to her. How did she always know when he was lying? It's not like he wasn't capable of being hard core. For all she knew, that threat could have been real. Sometimes it irritated him that Sophia seldom ever responded to his attempts to intimidate her. But most of the time, she just made Alastar laugh. His peers had frequently asked Alastar why he tolerated her, and honestly he didn't know. She was such an insignificant little squeak. She really shouldn't matter to him at all.

Alastar led the girls out to Middle field where there truly was *down falling* from the sky. Apparently, some of the older killers were practicing with their sniper rifles by bringing down geese from their perches high up the mountain. Two geese fell into the field within minutes of their arrival.

Demsie danced over to collect them. She took them by the necks and brought them back to Alastar and Sophia, already plucking the feathers off as she skipped. "I can share them with you." She told Alastar, because she knew that he was in charge.

It was incredibly tempting, but Sophia had been talking as though they had urgent business to attend to. She said that they had to go and case out the Burrow, in order to find out about the scrawny kid. "Save some for us." He told Demsie. "You should lay low until we swing by to escort you home, these woods are full of predators. Are you sure that you'll be safe here alone?"

Demsie just smiled and reached for the sky. Spinning in slow circles knee high in daisies as the sunlight filtered onto her cheeks. *She's not at all bad enough to survive here for long,* Alastar thought to himself.

They left Demsie to her fat geese and her flowery meadow. The sight of Demsie so happy put Alastar ill at ease. He wasn't sure why, maybe it was because that type of simple happiness wasn't a luxury that he had ever indulged himself in. Was he jealous of her? If so how could that be, when he knew that Demsie, sooner or later was going to end up dead?

The thought of Demsie's death made him somewhat unsettled. On the day that Demsie dies, Sophia was going to go absolutely ape. And Alastar knew with certainty that he didn't want Sophia to ever experience that, which was a curiosity to him. He thought about the ethical dynamics. Even though Alastar knew that he had been born evil, and had been raised entirely to do evil, he still felt slightly troubled that Sophia might lose a friend. Shouldn't he have been more coldhearted than that?

"It was nice of you to take Demsie to Middle Field." Sophia broke the silence.

"Well it might not be a favor to her if somebody finds her there. She should bunker herself down instead of dancing in the flowers."

Sophia was silent for a while as they walked. "I want to dance." She said. "Someday I'm going to be happy, and I'll dance like Demsie."

"Not when anyone's watching I hope, if you want to stay alive." Alastar hadn't ever heard Sophia speak with such a disregard for caution. He glanced back at her to check her mood and found that she was looking at him.

"You could be watching. When I do it, I mean. When I dance."

Alastar smiled at her. "Yeah, that would be funny to see."

"We could be happy together." She said.

"Why not? What's there to not be happy about?" He peeked back at her and saw the delicate corners of her mouth twitch downward, just for a moment.

"Anyways, thanks for being nice." She said.

"Always happy to help." Alastar lied. "Now, I think that we should jog for a while if we're gonna be able to case out the Burrow and find out about that skinny ghost of a kid. Why did you think he'd be at the Burrow anyways?" The two of them started to trot along the trail.

"I don't know, I think it was something that I smelled."

"That's weird." Alastar said softly as he jumped over a fallen log.

"Yeah. It is."

They ran for over an hour before Alastar called a halt. "We can stop here for a bit until you catch your breath." He told Sophia.

She nodded at him, her dark eyes always watching him from behind her thick black bangs. Alastar looked back at her and wondered why it was that he had first grown fond of her. His stare made her look away, but not for long. When she had caught her breath, she asked a question. "Do you think I'm pretty?"

Alastar wondered how that mattered to their mission, but he was smart enough to not say it. "There's not much to you Soph, but what there is, is pretty."

Sophia laughed a little laugh that gurgled like a boat's engine bubbling to life. "I know." She said, and she smiled.

They walked the rest of the way to the Burrow, and Alastar showed Sophia where they could go to get a peak at what was going on inside. Strangely, the old man had given Alastar a grand tour of the facility, including hidden hallways and entrances to the place. Even stranger was that he remembered it. The buried halls were like catacombs, connecting the Burrow's rooms into an indecipherable maze. A maze for which Alastar seemingly knew the key.

He couldn't remember anything other than receiving a brief tour from the old man, which in itself was strange enough, but it also seemed that he had developed a deep familiarity with the layout of this bunkered hive.

Security around the bunker was non-existent. No cameras, and not a soul around, just dim lights and carved rock, up until they heard the voices.

Alastar signaled all stop. The two of them strained to make out what was being said inside the echoing chamber far up the hall. *Follow me*, Alastar signaled with his hand. He didn't lead her towards the voices though. He wanted to hear them, but some instinct told him to take a path that ran perpendicular to the one that the voices were coming from. After a bit Alastar and Sophia turned, and then turned again, until their trail dead-ended into an area roughly the size of a closet. There they scaled silently up the wall about twelve feet, using notches that were barely evident in the rough stone.

The voices were strong there. They were coming from a crack in the rock. It was a crack just big enough to fit a very small squeak of a girl. Alastar signaled for Sophia to go on ahead and establish a visual on the speakers. She wriggled into the cool blackness with absolute silence. Meanwhile, Alastar settled into place to listen.

"You must hide your motion more carefully. If they realize what you are doing, you will die." It was an adult's voice, whiny and wavering.

"I thought he did quite well for his first day. Surely you did not learn mosquito instantly?" It was another adults voice, this one with a Dutch accent.

"I did not need to learn mosquito in one day." The first man said, his voice tinged with irritation. "But young Devant here, does."

"He absolutely does not. We could refine his training and insert him in with the residents in a couple of months. I propose that we train him longer, and go in with him as his special counselors. This way we could complete the rest of his training. I tell you, the fact that he was seen today should change nothing." The Dutch man's voice rose steadily as he found his passion.

A long silence.

"Devant, how many saw you?" The whiny voice spoke.

"Only him and the two girls." Devant's voice seemed young, but it was still tinged with ice. Something about it made Alastar suspect that the young speaker, would be both cunning and formidable.

"They will never question it."

"Then let us go from here." The Dutchman said. "The crude violence of this place disgusts me. We shall bring Devant back more ready and show these animals how delicately this game can be played."

"Indeed." The whiny voice agreed. "I already have something in mind for young Devant's grand entrance. These killers will be crapping themselves in fear, once our prodigy enters into their stunted society."

EIGHT

"What the hell is that?"

"You never seen a dog before, Josh?" Pax said.

"I've never seen a dog running free around the Station before. Just attack dogs trained to eat your ugly stupid face off." Josh said. The animal sniffed around some rocks on the forest's edge.

"What's a Golden Retriever doing here?" Yari said as his cold eyes trained onto man's best friend.

"It's Sneak and Prank's dog. They've been keeping it in that empty underground storage cache near the river, out past the artillery range." Pax said. Everyone had recently stopped using Pete and Hank's first names and they were now known by their monikers.

Josh bent and threw a rock towards the dog, but it landed a fair bit short and off to the right. The dog barely noticed. "What are they going to do with it?"

Pax laughed. "They just feed it, and they're training it. I think its part of a prank where they arm the dog with explosives and send it to blow something up. He's not supposed to be free, though. Those idiots musta left the door open."

"We should kill it." Yari sounded eager.

Just then the door burst open beside them. It was Alastar, he was finally done with his combat fencing session. Josh had noticed that Alastar often did a little extra training to keep his edge over the other guys, which also meant that they usually had to wait for him. Josh was just about to complain when he noticed the blood.

Alastar was walking with a damned knife handle sticking out of his thigh, and the blood had soaked his clothes, all the way down to his ankle. "What the —"

One angry glance from Alastar and Josh chose quickly to hold his tongue. Josh could see the beads of sweat all around Alastar's eyes, and the stifled grimace every time he bore weight through the wounded leg. Alastar was wincing with each step, even though he was using a seven-foot Zulu spear as a crutch.

Wisely, the other guys kept their mouths shut. Well, Yari and Pax did anyways, but Pete the sneak had just rounded the corner. Instances of Pete having good judgment were much like Hispid hare sightings, rare and fleeting. Pete proceeded to do what Pete did, which was to salt every wound and slap every burn that he saw. Alastar's wound couldn't have been missed.

"Studor's balls, you let someone stab you right up to the hilt. Shit, your supposed to win the fights, not make the rest of us feel better." Pete laughed. Right up until he realized that nobody else was laughing, especially Alastar. Pete humbled his demeanor quickly. "Um, It's just a joke. You know, because you always win the fights?"

"I didn't win this one. Someone gave Bartus a knife. A live blade, and I didn't see it until after I felt it."

"What did you do?" Pete said.

"I finished the fight, grabbed this damn spear to use as a crutch, and then walked out here to find you buncha heavy breathers waiting in ambush to heckle me?"

The tone of Alastar's voice made Josh feel that he needed to offer an explanation. "Ah. The three of us were just here looking at Pete's pet dog." Josh pointed to the retriever. "We didn't know you got — how your fight ended."

Pete the sneak and Alastar looked at the dog with the same curiosity that the others had earlier. Then everyone looked at Pete.

He cleared his throat. "Me and Prank found him about six weeks back. Not sure how he got onto Station grounds, but he's just a normal doggie." Pete took a few steps towards his dog, slapped his hands on his thighs and called out to it. "Come'ere Snoopy, come'ere boy."

The dog was smart enough to recognize his new Station name. He lifted his head and when he saw Pete, he barked once and started to run towards him.

He didn't get far though, maybe twenty five feet or so when a Zulu spear fell from the sky like a vengeful god's lightning bolt, taking the dog through the front of it's chest. The spear penetrated the dog's thorax like it was made of butter and buried it's sharp point into the soft ground underneath, deep enough that Snoopy didn't even tip sideways. With his heart impaled, the dog offered not even a twitch of life, allowing the corpse to remain perfectly upright, frozen in mid-stride by the spear that bisected his chest. The retriever stayed statuesque for several moments before the dog's head finally lolled off to the side.

Josh looked at Pete to gauge the sneak's reaction. He saw pretty much what he had expected to see. Nothing. Pete was a proper psychopath, and the dog's fate would mean almost as little to him as it would mean to Alastar. "Nice throw." Josh said to Alastar.

Yari was more excited though. "Are you kidding? Studor's balls! That throw was more than nice; it was stellar! Damn, we were gonna kill it anyways, but not like that. I wonder how long it'll stay in that position? I hope nobody touches it."

Other Station residents seemed to be wondering the exact same thing. They were beginning to gather around the skewered carcass in order to pay respects to the awesomeness of its execution.

They stared at it, they shook their heads in disbelief, and they murmured to themselves as they pointed towards Alastar. Nobody dared touch it. They all knew that Snoopy's carcass wasn't a dead body, as much as it was a monument.

A monument to the legend of Alastar Daivi.

When the day finally arrived for Alastar to witness the return of the illustrious Devant, even he had to admit that it was not a disappointment. A vast line up of cars was cruising slowly down the lonely road, which connected the Station with the outside world. They were all jet black and chrome, revealing a flamboyance rarely seen in the sober environment of the Station's grounds.

In the cars wake came the familiar sight of an armored van, which had been scratched and dented by both gunfire and shrapnel. It prowled slowly onto the central tarmac of Pod two and stopped at an angle. As the residents were still gathering to take in the sight, some keepers threw open the heavy side door with a metallic clang.

Men in black scrambled out from the van like commandos, readying their weapons, and pointing them back towards the van's open door. Even as that was happening, more men were bursting out of the other black cars in the caravan. All together, the Keepers were flashing more firepower than a Columbian cartel at a festival.

Alastar could see that his Station peers were impressed, but he also knew the show for what it was, a performance. Alastar smiled as he recognized one man as the Dutchman, based on Sophia's drawings of him. He climbed out of the van slowly, with casual self-importance and assumed an easy posture. Alastar continued to watch the vehicle. The guy that got out next, had to be the counselor with the whiny voice. He was a twitchy man who compulsively fondled the handle of his briefcase, with both of his hands.

Alastar wondered if there would be a drum roll for what would happen next. Orders were barked and three men hauled a heavily chained and manacled youth, out from the van. Devant was standing calmly despite his shackles, stink-eyeing the crowd of Keepers and residents as though he wanted to rip all of their heads off.

Alastar felt that the Keepers played their part well, as they handled Devant cautiously, despite the boy's outrageous restraints. It was as though this skinny kid were a two hundred fifty pound master assassin, when in fact; Devant was actually a hundred pound kid; and that, only when counting the weight of his chains.

Alastar looked at the crowd. He could almost see the respect that was being birthed amongst the Station residents, for this new kid who needed an armed escort and heavy chains, in order to suppress his lethal nature. They all seemed to believe the lie that Devant was in fact, an evil son-of-a-bitch.

Alastar watched the residents growing tense as the Dutchman plunged his long silver key into one of Devant's padlocks. It opened with a deadly click, which they had somehow gotten to sound like the sliding bolt of an assault rifle.

By that point, true or not, Alastar was absolutely loving the show, with Devant's arrival being the most wonderfully unique theatrical experience of the year. Alastar watched as Devant's cool eyes floated past him once, and the chained prisoner showed no trace of annoyance as he took in Alastar's wry grin. Of course not getting any reaction disappointed Alastar deeply, so he blew Devant an air kiss.

That did the trick. Devant's sadistic maniac guise wavered for just an instant, which was enough to show Alastar that the new kid was vulnerable. It didn't take long though, before Devant's surprise was replaced by a different and perhaps more sincere, homicidal stare. That was more like it.

Alastar met the gaze.

Once all of Devant's chains had been unbuckled, the guards backed away from him cautiously, and in one clean no doubt choreographed movement, Devant shrugged off all of his chains. The clattering links piled up at Devant's feet and everybody watching stepped back just a little, except for Alastar.

Devant smiled as he assessed his new neighbors slowly, nodding to some and issuing long uncomfortable stares towards others.

The monster was free of his chains and now everyone was wondering, why? If he was so dangerous, why was he being allowed to wander loose amongst them? Devant however, held his place and didn't move.

For a while, the tension built. Then, when people were starting to give up on the idea of Devant doing anything, he simply walked into the crowd of residents that was gathered to witness his spectacular arrival. People scrambled to step aside as quickly as they could, but it wasn't possible for everyone to clear out of Devant's path.

Alastar saw nothing more than the bump of a shoulder and then maybe the brush of an arm against Devant's sleeve, but when Devant emerged from the other side of the crowd, four residents lay dead on the ground. As still as stone. The deceased turned out to be Banger, Nucks, Bertie, and Sandra. Alastar would miss none of them.

Recognizing what had just happened, a low grade panic broke out amongst the residents as they jostled to give Devant sufficient space. Devant himself showed no signs of anxiety, though. In fact, he looked back at the path that he had just walked, and seemed to be almost surprised by the presence of the corpses.

"Oh Devant." The whining man said before he officiously checked for pulses on each body, shaking his head after he confirmed the loss. Then he faced the slim, dark haired boy head on. "We talked about this, remember?"

The Dutchman strode towards his colleague. "Come now Doctor, we have to expect at least some lapses, now and then. We will address this issue during his next counseling session. For now, let the boy be free to go and play. He needs to meet his new friends."

The Dutchman's words cleared the area of residents quicker than releasing a weaponized biohazard. It seemed that none of the children wanted to play with Devant. None of them, except for Alastar. He walked slowly up to Devant and stood in front of him. "So you're deadly." Alastar said. "So what?"

Devant smiled and said nothing.

Alastar walked in a slow circle around the new boy, and he was surprised when Devant let Alastar walk behind him. "You don't fear me at all." Alastar said.

Devant finally spoke. "I can make you dead whenever I choose to."

Alastar smiled at him. "I believe you. You have special training that most of us don't have." Devant's smug grin only broadened. Alastar was happy to see the smile though. He hoped that Devant's confidence might swell up to the point where the slightest prick could burst the whole bubble. Then Alastar slapped his hand suddenly against his own neck. "Ouch." He said. "Mosquito."

Alastar turned on the ball of his foot and walked away. He could almost hear Devant deflating behind him. His new pod-mate was a balloon rapidly hemorrhaging pride, all because Alastar had used the word, *mosquito*. It was the word that he had heard the Dutchman say back in the Burrow, when he and Sophia had been spying on them. The word meant nothing to Alastar beyond its typical usage, but the counselors had given it significance. *I thought he did quite well for his first day. Surely you did not learn mosquito instantly*?

Now the three of them would be wondering if Alastar was somehow less in the dark than they had originally thought. It would cause them concern, and Alastar wanted Devant to sweat. He wanted him to wonder if perhaps Alastar might have special training as well. Two could easily play at games of fear and theatrics, and soon Alastar would see how vulnerable Devant was.

Alastar was feeling very good as he walked back to his barracks. Devant's greeting had gone exceptionally well. He found himself pleased by all of it, except for the gnawing truth that Devant had the ability to kill instantly, and without any sign of violence. Fast, deadly, and able to disappear into shadows in the broad daylight? It was a formidable set of gifts. Devant would be Alastar's first seemingly supernatural foe. Alastar expected that the game ahead of him would be entertaining, but he would really hate to end up like Nucks, who was even uglier in death than he had been in life.

NINE

He can get so handsome, every time he laughs. Sophia looked at Alastar's blurred outline through a haze of tears that had been refreshingly birthed from laughter. Then Josh made the face again and the whole group of them howled some more.

Not to be outdone though, Hank the prank stood ramrod straight, puffed out his chest, and with his best Commander Studor imitation said, "Mr. Codfish, er I mean Mr. Daivie, would you please —." Hank started to lose his composure as the other kids crumpled one by one, into hysterics. His stern voice softened as he tried to stifle a smile. "If you pleee-hee-heeeease —." Then Hank lost it and he became undone by laughter as well.

But by that point Josh was back on task. "Mr. Daivie, if you hadn't been *helping* Bartus with the navigation, do you still believe that he would have ended up running the rapids, ass first?" That was enough for them all to lose control once again.

Mercifully for Sophia, over time the jokes finally began to ebb, and they were all left staring at each other red eyed, defying each other to crack another joke.

But the moment of levity had past, and sobriety prevailed once again. "Why do the higher ups call you Codfish anyways?" The question was Pete's.

"I don't know." Alastar said.

I know. Lately, Sophia had been mentally grinding out whether she should tell him. COD was a loose code for *Child Of Destiny*. She knew that of course, she had always known that. But Sophia wondered though how the higher ups had known it.

Then Demsie stood up and walked in a circle. "Codfish, codfish jump off your plate, angels speak of destiny. That is not your fate." Then she collapsed to the floor, balled herself up, and cried softly.

Everyone in the room burst into laughter once again, except for Sophia.

Sophia felt a cold shiver go through her like a blast of winter wind, but she knew the others would never notice it.

"Even that new kid, Devant, calls you Codfish." Pax said. "From him, it sounds like an insult though. I think something should be done about that."

Sophia watched as Pax began to grind his teeth the way he always did when he was musing about violence.

Alastar seemed to be stifling more laughter. *He thinks that Pax is a fool.* "Well Pax, you're welcome to defend my honor whenever you like. I'm sure Devant will be receptive to whatever form of mayhem you plan to unleash upon him. Mind yourself though, I don't think that he'll fight fair."

Pax's brow furrowed. "Yeah, that's true. He's a dirty little trickster. Maybe we should plan things out a little bit before we erase him."

"That's just what I intend." Alastar said. Sophia watched as Alastar pulled himself to his feet, then he flashed a piercing glance towards her. Sophia felt her breath catch just a little bit in anticipation. "You coming pip-squeak?"

She shot to her feet and rushed towards him, barely managing to slow herself to a walk before running into him.

Once they were outside, Alastar asked her in a low voice. "Why do you think they call me Codfish?"

"Destiny." She said simply, not really wanting to go into it because Alastar never believed things like that anyways.

Then a voice called from behind. "Sophia!" *It was Demsie.* Sophia glanced back to see her running towards them. When she caught up, Demsie was slightly flushed. "You left me with the killers." Her voice was ragged and tears rimmed her eyes.

"I'm sorry, Demsie." Sophia kissed her lightly on the cheek. Suddenly Sophia felt overwhelmed with emotion and her own eyes sprouted tears as well. She hugged Demsie desperately.

"Um, ladies, this is a bit much. We only walked fifty feet. Look at Demsie, she's fine right? Sophia, I'm sure that Demsie has already forgiven you. So can we keep walking now?"

Sophia looked at Alastar, but what she saw wasn't only him. He was a battleground. Battle raged in the sky above him and on the earth at his feet. Then all at once the big white man was there, and a power crackled off of him like several suns. Sophia pulled free of Demsie's grasp, and ran.

Do not fear, the words resounded in her head, pressing on her like the voice of her own doom echoing through the cosmos. It was the voice that made her run that much faster. Sophia knew in her heart that she had no choice, and that running was her only option. There was just so much power. Too much. Far too much for a small girl to be around.

Suddenly Sophia felt herself getting jerked to a stop. It was Alastar, he had grabbed her, but she kicked him and clawed at him to be free. The fear was growing and growing within her like something alive.

Alastar had her physically subdued though, and the COD was whispering something. Sophia felt like an animal in a trap as she looked back at the huge man that was standing over Demsie like a tower. Why didn't she run from him? Then Sophia saw Demsie reached out to the man. "Demsie, no!" Sophia's voice sounded shrill, even to her. Her cry was at an octave that only stark terror could produce.

She felt the hard pressure of Alastar's hand clamping over her mouth, so Sophia whipped her head side to side, fighting to break free. She had lost sight of Demsie for the moment, and couldn't get his hand away from her mouth, so she maneuvered the finger into position and bit it.

"Ouch! Dammit Sophia. What the hell?" Alastar pushed her away and shook the pain from his finger. He looked down at it briefly, long enough to see that Sophia had drawn blood. When Sophia realized that she was free again, she ran.

This time she ran for a long while. Out of the pod, and into the open spaces. Over that time her panic was gradually stilled through the comforting rhythm of her steps. The exertion was therapeutic to her, and it calmed her terror, giving her heart rest.

Soon her head was clear, and Sophia was able to think about what had happened. Sophia began to feel bad for biting Alastar, but she hadn't had a choice at the time. She had to get away, and Alastar was restraining her.

Soon Sophia reached the woods. It was dangerous for her to be out there on her own, but she wasn't ready to go back yet. She needed to keep running.

Minutes later she heard what sounded like a twig snapping behind her. Sophia looked back and saw nobody there. Of course she knew that there was someone there, and she felt that she also knew who, so she kept on running.

Sophia traveled deeper and deeper into the forest, underneath the towering pines that had spent decades reaching heavenwards, and past the broad ferns that covered the forest floor like fur. Sophia could feel the comforting pulse of the land there. It was an ancient land and it felt good to her. Of course there had been death there as well, generations of death.

Sophia kept running.

Soon she heard his footsteps fall into sync with hers, he would be just a few feet behind her, so close to her, sharing the same gait. It gave her goose bumps.

Sophia didn't look back at him though, which actually took most of her self-control. She felt an urge to stop running and grab his torso. She wanted to cry into his chest and kiss his bleeding finger, and apologize again and again, but no killer would ever understand that type of behavior. Not yet.

Instead, she allowed herself to slow to a walk and Alastar fell in beside her. She did steal one glance up at him. He rolled his eyes back at her. She could almost hear his thoughts. *Crazy Oracles, so unreliable.* But there was fondness in the gesture. Alastar would have also be wondering how long until his association with Sophia would get him killed. Then she felt a blanket of shame fall upon her, and she turned away.

Tears formed in her eyes. It was always the tears that the killers hated most when it came to oracles, unless of course it was the killers that had caused the tears. Then they were always delighted to see them. To Sophia though, tears weren't good or bad. They were just tears, an honest expression of something natural. She felt his hand brush her shoulder lightly.

"Sophia. It's okay. It's just the drugs that they give you guys."

For some reason that she didn't comprehend, those simple words made Sophia's composure break. She turned to him, not caring anymore if he saw her tears, and she shouted. "No! It's more than the drugs. It's me, don't you see? Of course you don't, but I do. It's the world too, and how it's put together, there are scary things that you don't even know about!"

Alastar held his hands up and spoke calmly. "Settle down Sophia, it's okay now."

Then all at once, something shifted their focus. They were both instantly aware that they were no longer alone. Alastar spun around and Sophia melted into his shadow. It was fourteeners, three of them, standing right there, and it would have been impossible not to notice that they were carrying sticks.

Their leader was Smacks, a rangy teen who had hit his growth spurt early. He was famous for his dry wit and his unrivaled narcissism. *Smacks loves Smacks better than Tracker loves tracks.* That was a saying out of Pod five. It was a stupid saying really. Tracker was there as well, and it was a complete lie that Tracker loved tracks. In fact, Tracker was a terrible tracker. Reports were that he would have barely been able to find himself on a sand beach.

That humbling truth, along with the Station resident's apparent love of the saying, made Tracker something of a local joke. A joke not often told to his face, though. The reason that people were careful was because Tracker was exceptionally cruel, stemming not only from his unfortunate name, but also because of his stunted growth. Despite being four years older than her, the fourteener was not very much bigger than Sophia. By nature Tracker was also petty, and Sophia knew it. So she was careful not to make any eye contact with him.

The third fourteener was hanging back a bit. That kid was named Silent Steve, and he spoke only in whispers, when he spoke at all. Sophia knew very little about Steve but when she looked at him, she saw a fire burning in his chest. Strange.

"Hello Smacks." Alastar smacked the name.

Smacks' devilishly handsome features twisted into a smile. "Hello, Alastar Daivi." Mouthing Alastar's last name theatrically.

"Looking good, as always." Alastar said.

"Thank you, runt. A compliment always sounds better coming from someone as — notable, as the Legend."

Sophia watched as Alastar ignored the sarcasm and kicked at the ground sheepishly. "Aw shucks." Alastar mimed being bashful, it was clearly disingenuous.

Behind Smacks, Sophia could see Tracker's temper flaring up. Alastar's defiance was subtle, and in the Station, subtle often got you respect. But his response was a fine line from mockery, and mockery usually got you bloodied. She hoped that Alastar had some type of plan other than to stomp on these cobra's tails.

She never could tell with him. Her boy often moved from brilliant strategy to foolhardy risk, in the space of a breath. It was that unpredictable nature of his, that sometimes led others to proceed with caution when they were around him. But right now, her and Alastar were seriously outmuscled, and in this instance she desperately hoped that Tracker's ire would not overpower his sense of caution.

Luckily Smacks seemed to be the leader, and he chose to laugh at Alastar. "Hey, you're all right kid. I think that we could be friends, of sorts."

Sophia watched Smacks as he talked. She could hear the kindness of his words and the expert control of how he used his vocal tone, but all Sophia could see when she looked at him, was the cloud of lies wafting off of his scalp like a stench.

This one was clever, almost cerebral. She hoped that Alastar would be careful, if he knew what was best.

"Okay then." Alastar said. "We're friends." Then he moved to go, grabbing Sophia by the hand. There was no such thing as friends in the Station.

Smacks stepped in front of him. "Wait, what's the hurry? We just got to talking."

Alastar stopped. "It's true. Where are my manners?" Sophia gave a quick glance towards Tracker, who was getting madder by the minute.

"No harm, Legend. We can all get a little bit hasty from time to time. It's not in a killer's nature to be idle, is it?" With Smacks' winning smile and his seemingly warm sentiment, he could have almost passed for kind, but then his true nature was revealed. "For example, that week all those years ago. The one when you were absent for all your training blocks, I'm sure that you weren't on vacation then, were you?"

Failing miserably at hiding her emotions, Sophia's eye's flared, and all the killers saw it. *Studor's balls*, she would have to learn some self control someday. Inwardly berating herself, even Sophia felt frustration at her oracle's temperament. At the moment she was anyways.

The time away from training that Smacks was referencing was of course years ago, when Alastar had been taken to the Burrow. Back when it had happened, everyone had noticed that he was gone. Some even thought for a while that he had died. Then, when he showed up alive it created all kinds of speculation. Now Smacks was picking at the secret, and he was doing it as indelicately as she would have expected an egomaniac killer who held the power position, to do it.

Alastar said nothing.

"The reason that I ask is quite simple really. That story is the only peculiar occurrence in your whole entire miserable life, that hasn't been entered into the Alastar Daivi legend. I've got an idea though," Smacks smiled. "How about you tell us, just for the fun of it, and you can save yourself a brutal beating with these sticks."

On cue, Tracker smacked the ground with his thick club-like tree limb.

Alastar was silent for a while. Sophia knew that he would be weighing his options. She also knew that if anyone could negotiate his way out of this, it would be Alastar. In the meantime though, the butterflies in her stomach were a whirlwind of fear. Sophia reminded herself that Alastar would try to keep her safe if he could. If he couldn't though, this could get incredibly bad, rapidly.

Smacks didn't rush Alastar to speak. In fact, he was delighting in the control position that he held over the situation.

Sophia looked up at Alastar. The line of his chin was smooth and he was gently chewing at his lower lip, apparently thinking about Smacks' offer.

Sophia knew that Alastar wouldn't tell him about the Burrow. He hadn't told anyone. Whenever someone asked him he always said that he couldn't remember, but he had to remember, didn't he? Since when do people forget entire weeks of their life, and Alastar remembered most things better than anyone.

"I'll tell." Alastar said. Sophia stared at him in shock. "I'll tell silent Steve."

Sophia watched closely for Smacks' reaction, and she saw his emotions play out in sequence. At first Smacks experienced a moment of frustration, and then a time of consideration. That was followed by resignation, and then he moved back to frustration again. Sophia had no idea why Alastar had chosen to say what he did, but she knew that there was always a reason, and judging by Smacks' reaction, it must have been a clever play.

When nobody offered a response, Alastar gave Sophia a gentle nudge towards the trees. Then he stepped sideways, closer to Tracker who instantly flared with anger when Alastar moved into his proximity.

Smacks hadn't moved or said anything.

"But I won't tell Steve anything with this puny scrap of Tracker scat anywhere near me. He smells like shit and I don't trust how he prattles on behind your back." Alastar said to Smacks. "If I tell him, he'll just take the credit and make you and me out to be fools."

Then Alastar turned and spoke softly to Tracker, but Sophia couldn't make out what he was saying. Suddenly, Tracker swung his wooden club at Alastar with all of his strength. It was a clumsy attack. Sophia knew that Alastar had more than enough skill and speed to move in close and stuff the assault, but he didn't do that. Instead Alastar retreated, backing towards Smacks.

"Tracker stop! I'm sorry!" Alastar said, his eyes were pinned wide. Tracker swung again. This time the fat knob of wood at the end of Tracker's stick just barely missed Alastar's smooth chin. "Stop!" He said again.

The next attack happened fast, too fast for Sophia to see it clearly. Tracker swung the club in a wide arc, but this time Alastar seemed unable to dodge it. Losing his balance, he stumbled clumsily into Tracker just as the club was gaining momentum. Sophia watched as Alastar's supposed misstep made him crash into Tracker's swinging arms. Then Alastar's head banged into Tracker's brow, splitting the skin above the ornery little killer's eye. After that, Alastar fell to the ground as though the blow had dazed him.

Just then a horrible sound echoed throughout the woods. Smacks was crying out with a carnal scream that contained equal parts pain and rage. When Sophia looked towards the noise, it wasn't hard to figure out why Smacks had screamed. Tracker's club lay at Smacks' feet, and it was stained in blood.

Smacks' blood. Smacks the narcissist whose perfect aquiline nose was now horribly bent and deeply cut. Blood poured from the ugly gash on the big fourteener's nose and into the killer's mouth, staining Smacks' teeth red, with carnivorous bloodlust.

Smacks' scream got Tracker's attention instantly. And that growing cloud of rage had Tracker backing away from the much larger killer, even before Smacks made the decision to advance on him. A moment later, an all out pursuit began through the trees. Soon they disappeared. Sophia had no doubt that Smacks would get his revenge, immediately or eventually.

Alastar picked himself up from the ground and gestured for Sophia to come close. She didn't hesitate in obeying. Alastar turned, and was beginning to walk away with her when silent Steve spoke.

It was a whisper. "It's unlike Tracker to be so clumsy, letting go of his club in mid swing." Steve let the comment take on a weight of it's own. Alastar looked back at Steve. "You still owe me a story, Legend."

Alastar nodded to him. The gesture was almost respectful. "How about we just say I owe you? Is that a deal?"

Steve smiled.

Sophia was overjoyed to be walking away from that area of the forest.

She followed Alastar along the trail that led back to the Station barracks. He had won. Once again, he had won. How did he know to do the things that he did? She suspected that even Alastar didn't know the answer to that. The important thing was that he always won, and he always kept her safe.

Sophia reached forward and grabbed his hand. He didn't pull away from her, and she cried.

TEN

Sophia knew that she had to confront him, but she didn't want to sound needy, or like a possessive little bitch. That was the biggest problem, because Sophia was needy, and possessive, and just about every other emotional thing that could get on a killer's nerves. The best thing she could do was to stay silent.

Sophia breathed. Yes, she would have control, and say as little as she could. But what if she saw things going wrong, subtle things. Small things. Things that were real but would sound insignificant if she were to speak them out loud.

Sophia breathed again. All she had to do was stay quiet.

Sophia's barracks door clattered open and Alastar strode in, grinning. Sophia ran to him and hugged his chest. "I thought you might be dead." She said. What? No she hadn't. Not at all in fact. "I mean not dead really, I feared it but I didn't think it. Honest. But you've got more and more enemies Alastar. I mean —." Then she cut herself off. Sophia had sworn herself to silence. Alastar was looking at her curiously.

She pushed away from him, forced a smile. Sophia unclenched her hands and let her shoulders relax, she needed a new subject. "So how was your day and what have you been up to?" Small talk? Even as she said it, Sophia was kicking herself. Psychopaths didn't do small talk; once again it was her neediness talking for her.

"I was with Desda." Alastar said.

"That bitch? Why?"

Alastar was looking at her. An eyebrow was raised but he wasn't speaking. Studor's balls, Sophia wanted to run from her own barracks. Just then she spotted Demsie at the door a few feet behind Alastar.

"Demsie!" Sophia said, grateful for the distraction.

"Why are the both of you so bracketed?" Demsie said, making air quotes with her fingers. "Emotions are just like air if you only breathe them."

By degrees of magnitude, she was more womanly than any of the girls Alastar's age. She had a dangerously distracting shape, and no doubt a cold ruthless heart to go with it. For months now she had been treating Alastar with something that felt suspiciously like kindness.

Although it seemed strange, truthfully Alastar was welcoming of it. He was happy to have another ally now that Bartus, Devant, and Smacks all had it out for him.

Desda was as smart as she was gorgeous and distracting. And she was always noticing things, small things. Helpful things. Desda often gave him information, and she asked nothing for it. That's why her manner had to be called kindness, but Sophia wasn't quick to accept her. She must have been jealous because Desda had boobs and she didn't.

Nice boobs too, as Josh never seemed to tire of pointing out. Aside from those highly noticeable assets, another good thing about Desda was that she seemed to take a sincere interest in Alastar as a person. She really wanted to know who he was, and she asked him questions that nobody had ever bothered to ask. Sometimes Alastar even surprised himself by how much he enjoyed answering those questions.

It seemed, that Desda simply loved to listen, and the more she listened, the easier it got for Alastar to tell her things.

Desda expressed kindness easier than most of the other Station killers, perhaps that was due to her training as a nurse in the infirmary. Also, when she wasn't caring for the sick and injured, she helped out as a librarian's assistant, shuffling books from shelf to shelf. Two relatively noble professions to pursue, for a place like this.

From the first time that Alastar had taken notice of Desda, she had been a loner. Maybe that was because there were so few residents her age left alive in the pod. It was a situation for which Alastar in fact, held most of the blame. She had been a twelver when Alastar's land mine tactic had slaughtered her age-mates. Of course she didn't actually blame him. No psychopath could ever truly care enough to muster up any real sense of blame. To a killer; *dead was dead and gone was gone, and the dead were dead and gone.* Every Station resident knew those words by the time that they had turned four. And unlike the oracles that seemed to be put off by death, the killers honored those words as though they were scripture. The younger killers drew comfort from the saying, when the nights seemed cold and edged with danger and the morning sun was an eternity away.

Alastar had been musing on all of those things, when suddenly Devant appeared out of nowhere in front of him. Alastar shot to his feet in response. How the kid managed to skulk around so effortlessly, Alastar hadn't yet figured out, but lately it seemed that Devant was always close.

Several times now, Devant had demonstrated that he had a knack for the random taking of lives, which was why Alastar never stayed seated in the skinny killer's presence. Alastar straightened himself to full height. Dammit, Devant was getting taller than him.

Even worse, because of the way Devant could invisibly ghost himself from place to place, lately Alastar couldn't ever be certain that he was truly alone, and that was starting to get inside his head. He often found himself expecting Devant to materialize out of the ether, to put a quick end to the legend of Alastar Daivi. It didn't matter what subject block Alastar was in, or what time of the day it was, Devant could always make an appearance. As the world's boniest apparition, Devant seemed committed to haunting Alastar throughout his long days of training, with the kid never feeling all that far away at night either. Lately, Devant had been too much inside Alastar's head, and far too little in Alastar's sight.

Devant's grin shone in Alastar's face, from less than two and a half feet away, he was all teeth. Alastar watched his enemy carefully, looking for the slightest twitch of motion that would signal the attack, but Devant stood as still as stone.

"You've seemed on edge lately." Devant said.

"I've always been high strung for an assassin." Alastar said as he held Devant's gaze.

"That's not what I've heard about you. The legends of Alastar Daivie speak of a child that stares death in its ugly maw, and brazenly risks life and limb. They say he gambles with the reaper as though they were merely playing poker."

"Sometimes partially true. For example, I am staring at an ugly maw right now." Alastar waited for just a moment as his insult sunk in. "But isn't it a fool that believes everything that he hears? The truth is, I'm actually quite conservative."

Devant smiled as though the insult hadn't stung him, but Alastar knew that it had. Then he ran his spidery fingers casually through his hair. Alastar knew the gesture for what it was, Devant was stalling for time as he tried to compose himself. Only Alastar, being who he was, didn't plan on giving Devant the luxury of time. So he punched him.

Three hard blows landed and Devant's eyes shot wide with shock. Surely the spider couldn't have been all that surprised that Alastar had chosen offence instead of defense. Considering the circumstances, every Station raised kid that Alastar knew would have been pretty much expecting the assault. Hell, it was a miracle that they hadn't fought up until that time.

Devant flailed blindly as he retreated. Alastar knew that if he could get a decent hold on Devant's throat, he could end this threat forever. So Alastar swept Devant to the ground hard and dropped his weight onto Devant's skinny frame. He rolled Devant into position for a choke as he thought about how good it would feel to have all of this over with.

Suddenly, there was a burning sensation in Alastar's eyes, which nearly made him release his grip, but he knew that it was exactly what Devant wanted. So Alastar squeezed the skinny kid's throat even tighter, and tighter still. Devant's execution was going well until a searing pain lanced up Alastar's arm like lightning, weakening his grip despite Alastar's best efforts to hold the choke firm.

Then Devant regained his feet, fury burning in his eyes. "I should kill you." He breathed as the blood ran from his nose and mouth.

Alastar said nothing as he shook out his own useless, paralytic arm and regained his feet. Once again, pain lanced through the floppy limb. What the hell had Devant done to him?

Devant laughed. "That'll hurt for a week." Then he backed away and left.

Once Devant was gone, Alastar inspected his arm, every small movement brought with it a new sort of agony. He saw no bruising and it wasn't broken. There was no blood. Then he saw that on the outside of his arm just above the elbow, a little pin was stuck into him around the vicinity of the radial nerve. Could that be why it hurt so damn much? No, the pin was off of the nerve.

Alastar touched the tiny needle and the pain that resulted, shot all the way up to his temples. He staggered despite all of his resolve not to let anyone see that Devant had hurt him. How the hell do you take out a needle that you can't even touch? Anesthetic would help him, but if Alastar got medical help for it, the residents would all judge that Devant had won the skirmish.

Alastar looked closer at the needle. It was a wondrous little barb. How had he gotten it into Alastar's arm in the first place? The answer in one word, was obvious.

Devant.

Devant was an unfortunate mystery that Alastar didn't want or need intruding into his life right now, but his own situation was what it was. Alastar knew what he had to do. So he got down onto his knees just to be safe, clenched his teeth together, and pulled at the cruel barb. Like frozen fire burning away his soul, he was suddenly doused in the characteristic sensation of shock which often preceded agony. Then with all the grace of a tsunami, a massive barrage of pain signals buffeting his central nervous system, lighting up remote parts of his brain that hadn't been used since he had first been birthed. Somewhere deep in the primitive centers of his mind, a switch was flipped and Alastar passed out cold.

When his eyes flickered open he saw Desda approaching him from down the path. She had been moving silently and held a knife in her hand. When Alastar caught her in his sight, she startled. For a moment she stared at him blankly, and then her face lit up in a beautiful smile. She rushed to his side.

"Oh, I thought you were dead." She said as she gathered up Alastar's weakened body into her arms and pressed his head to her breast. Her ample breast. Alastar didn't move or speak. "What happened?"

"I'm fine." Alastar avoided answering her question.

"I'm so glad." She said as she pressed him harder into her soft bosom. He wondered if this behavior was somehow a by-product of her nursing training. Then Alastar saw Sophia. She was standing silently, watching from behind a bush.

Desda followed Alastar's gaze to the small dark haired girl that was so frequently Alastar's shadow. *She would have known that I was hurt*, Alastar thought. He watched as Desda smiled warmly towards Sophia, and continued to stroke Alastar's hair like a pet.

Too much like a pet.

Alastar pulled himself to his feet. His arm ached with the deepest, most all encompassing ache that Alastar had ever experienced, but the arm still felt better than when the needle had been in it. Alastar bent down to pick up the pin. It was just a pin, nothing special. He touched the tip to his tongue. Nothing.

When he looked back towards Sophia again, she was gone. Alastar found himself wondering what Sophia might know. The pin was a mystery. Was it special somehow or had the pain been from the way Devant had placed it? There was only one way to know for sure, so he took the pin and plunged it deep into his arm again. It hurt, but it was not out of the ordinary. When he pulled it out blood rose from the puncture wound.

Alastar glanced at Desda and she was smiling at him.

"I need to go." He told her.

Alastar walked back towards his Pod. He wanted some time to think about what had been happening lately. His position in the Station had been progressively weakening over the recent months. Alastar had too many enemies and it seemed that they were organizing themselves against him. Alastar needed to turn this situation around, soon. Somehow, Alastar knew that Devant would be the key.

Devant was strong in unexpected ways though, and he was clever. After what had just happened, Devant would be more careful in Alastar's presence, which would make taking him out a lot harder.

Deep down, Alastar knew that the answer needed to be strategic, not tactical, which was why Alastar needed some time to think. What was Devant's weakness?

Soon he found himself in Pod two where Josh was filing a piece of metal into a wicked point. "What's that?" Alastar said.

"Just a little project I'm working on." Josh replied. What are you up to?"

"I've got a project of my own. Unfortunately, it's more complex than a shank made out of razed metal can cure."

"So you're telling me that there's problems that razed metal *can't* cure?" Josh's smile always lightened Alastar's mood.

Alastar sat down beside him. "You should know it better than me, Josh. Aren't you the master of relationships?"

"Ha! Master of nothing more like, but I do keep my ear to the ground."

"So what do you hear about Devant?" Alastar said.

"As dangerous as he is bony. People here fear him. They think he's going to take you down."

"So what do you think? Will he take me down?"

"No. I don't think so. You're too smart for that. You'll find a way to exploit his biggest weakness."

"I will?" Alastar looked into his friend's eyes. They were as cold as any killers, but they held insight. "Which one of Devant's gaping weaknesses do you think I'll exploit?"

Josh smiled. "The only one that could get the job done, his counselors."

Alastar looked at Josh steadily, wondering what his allies criminally genius mind could see, that Alastar's mind did not. He had never considered the counselors to be a liability to Devant. But what did Josh see?

Devant was taken away several times per week for his *counseling*. Station residents believed that the counseling was all about trying to control Devant's darker urges, but Alastar wasn't buying that at all. For starters, why had Devant left him alive today? He had Alastar downed and weakened. If Devant gloried in the kill as much as the Station gossips suggested he did, he would have never left without stopping Alastar's heart first.

What were the counselors up to then? What was their end goal? For that matter, why was Devant transferred to the Station in the first place? In certain ways, the whole thing smelled like an act. Maybe that was Devant's Achilles heel, the fact that he was a fraud. The idea made Alastar smile.

Strategy, not tactics.

Stealth and subterfuge, not frontal assault. It would take time and planning. Hopefully Alastar could survive long enough to make it happen

CHAPTER ELEVEN

ELEVEN

The more Alastar thought about his situation, the darker his mood became. He carried out his training exercises with brutal efficiency. During that time he kept no one's council and for reasons beyond even his understanding, he grew angry at even friendly attempts to make conversation.

Alastar told himself that it was the gnawing ache in his arm that was making him disagreeable, and admittedly, his arm hurt like a bitch. It turned out that Devant was being conservative when he predicted that the arm would hurt for a week. It had been almost three weeks and the improvement in the pain was negligible.

His allies were all angry with him because of his moods, but they should have known to just leave him alone. Mostly it was Devant that pissed Alastar off. Devant, and his counselors. Quite simply, it was the fact that they existed that irritated him.

Alastar had found himself a window high up in the loft of one of Pod two's warehouse storage facilities. It gave him the seclusion that he desired, and a good view of the grounds. It became Alastar's habit to spend his hours up there whenever he wasn't training, just thinking and watching. Station residents had started calling it the COD's nest.

Every once in a while Devant or Bartus would walk by his nest, just to taunt him. Lacking any sense of subtlety, Bartus made obscene gestures at Alastar, while Devant merely smiled at him. Strangely, Smacks had a different strategy; he seemed to be avoiding the area, which bothered Alastar even more than the actions of the other two. Alastar had to wonder what Smacks might be up to.

He was watching the compound when Sophia and Demsie drifted past his loft, Sophia's eyes were turned up towards him. Alastar smiled for the first time in weeks when he first saw them. The two oracles had acquired a new nickname, a shared one that suited them perfectly.

Sophia was so spirited, and looked dark with her black hair and her Latina features. She was always ready to take action, even when it was none of her business.

Demsie though, was like water, refreshingly soft by nature, and easy-going. And unlike Sophia, Demsie's hair and skin were as white as snow. All of those things guaranteed them their nicknames. As Sophia and Demsie walked through the Station grounds, the two of them were pressed against one another, as they always were. Black against white, like the Daoist Yin and Yang symbol. Which was why Sophia was now named Yang and Demsie was now known as Yin.

As Alastar was watching the compound, he noticed Charlie strolling by while trying unsuccessfully to look casual. Something suspicious about Charlie's motion drew Alastar's eye like lightening to a rod. Charlie had grown larger over the last couple of years. You'd think that it might have given him a bit of respect from the other residents, but no. He was still the same annoying kid with the same annoying mouth, as he had been when they were all eighters, huddled together in the rain and expecting to die before the dawn.

Charlie seemed to be on an intercept course with Sophia and Demsie. Alastar's eyes did a quick tactical analysis of the yard. It couldn't be by coincidence that Bartus's allies seemed to be rounding almost all of the corners, and filtering into the compound. They were all looking far too casual to actually be casual. Alastar could have written the book from that point on.

He stood up.

Charlie reached out and grabbed Demsie by her blond hair and yanked her away from Sophia's side. Demsie gave a muted shriek and then fell into the dirt. She wasn't down long before Charlie scooped her up by her narrow waist and threw her to the ground again.

With her eyes wide with fear, Demsie tried to scramble away on hands and feet but Charlie fell on her in an instant. The killer stepped on the back of her leg, pinning her motionless like a rat with a boot on it's tail.

Alastar knew that he was being called out. He watched from his window as Sophia crouched in fear, fully expecting the assault to turn toward her at any moment, but unwilling to run away and abandon her friend. Alastar watched the entire drama from up in his COD's nest. He didn't intend to step into Bartus's crude trap in order to help Demsie, but he wondered if he would have been able to resist the urge to act, if they turned their hands against Sophia.

Why were they assaulting Demsie and not Sophia? The answer came to him almost as soon as the question formed in his mind. They were still afraid.

They knew that messing with Sophia could initiate a response on a different level than merely the rescue that they were baiting him into performing.

Alastar watched as Demsie was being beaten, and tears streamed down Sophia's face. Her dark eyes were moving from Alastar, who stood in his loft with his hands against the window, to the repeated buffeting of her friend. Sophia winced with each and every blow that Demsie suffered.

Then Charlie pulled out his cock.

This caused Alastar to reconsider what his response should be. Perhaps action would not have been imprudent. By not acting, it could even make Alastar look weak, and showing weakness in the Station had a way of leading ultimately to death.

Demsie was looking thoroughly bloodied when Charlie began to piss on her pure white hair.

Alastar made his decision. For now the damage was already done, and it couldn't be undone. There was damage to Demsie's body, Demsie's mind, and Demsie's heart, but most disturbingly, there was damage to Alastar's reputation.

Alastar had failed to act, which meant one of two things. Either Alastar was too weak to protect his property, or Demsie was not Alastar's property, which would leave her out in the cold. To protect Alastar's reputation though, it had to be the latter.

The players in the ambush all began to dissipate once they saw that Alastar was not going to walk into their trap. Alastar waited a few seconds until the yard was clearer, and then he made his way down from the COD's nest. He opened the front door of the warehouse just as Charlie was tapping the last drops of yellow off of his cock. Charlie smiled.

Alastar began walking towards Sophia who was crouched into a shivering ball on the ground. Her dark skin had blanched almost as white as Demsie's. Charlie's look was smug, but perhaps his celebration was premature because Alastar wasn't the only dangerous animal penned up in the Station's cage.

Looking past Charlie, Alastar saw Silent Steve step purposefully into the yard. He was looking at Demsie's small body, now colored all red and yellow, lying still on the ground. Just for a moment, Alastar thought that he saw Steve's face change.

What had that been? Whatever it was it had only been there for an instant. For a moment it might have looked like compassion, but then the cold mask fell over Silent Steve's features once again.

Alastar purposely ignored Steve's presence as he was walking over to Sophia. Alastar bent down, and lifted Sophia up like a sack of grain, claiming her. She grunted as her body landed roughly across his shoulder, and then Alastar turned to go.

Charlie was laughing because he knew that Alastar was going to do nothing about Demsie, but he still didn't dare saying anything. Neither did Silent Steve as he approached Charlie from behind, but then again, Steve seldom did.

As quiet as a cat, he approached. When he got close enough, silent Steve grabbed both of Charlie's shoulders and simultaneously drove the bottom of his heel down at a sharp angle into the outer side of Charlie's knee. Even a poplar trunk would have had a hard time withstanding that blow, and Charlie's knee did far worse than the tree trunk would have.

There was a loud popping sound, followed by howls of pain and cursing. Steve didn't care. He walked over to Demsie's bloodied frame and scooped her up in the same way that Alastar had grabbed Sophia.

Alastar assumed that Steve would take Demsie away with him, but instead Silent Steve spoke to him once again.

"Take this one too." Steve said as he walked over to Alastar and dropped Demsie's body onto Alastar's other shoulder. Demsie moaned weakly as Alastar shifted her into better position.

"Okay." Alastar said.

Silent Steve turned and left.

CHAPTER TWELVE

TWELVE

Since the incident, Alastar's moods had grown even darker. People were laughing at him from the far sides of rooms, and the seveners had even dared to chant a taunting song in his presence before they had scattered like the insects that they were.

He could have squished them, but it would only have stained his shoe.

As the days and weeks passed, the Station's social system was goading him into a response, but if Alastar were to offer an unbalanced response, it would be taken as an admission that he actually cared for Demsie. Then the belief that he cared for Demsie would weaken his authority even further, what little of it remained anyways. Questions would be asked like, *if he cares for her, why didn't he stop Charlie*? It was a no win scenario. Damn that girl for having complicated his life so much.

Josh and the boys had been avoiding him. They were all still sulking because Alastar had cut them out of the loop. The damn fools, they were acting like children, and acting your age was a deadly mistake in the Station. Studor had said it best, *Certainly our kids need to be physically and mentally advanced for their ages, we're not running a preschool. The experiences that we provide in the Station, are specially tempered to provide these young men and women with the insight they need to thrive in an increasingly harsh world.* Alastar had always remembered the Commander saying those words, in some ways it gave his entire existence purpose.

Sophia wasn't mad at him. The first thing she said to him, was that she understood why he had done what he did, but then she added that she wished he had done it differently. For some reason, that irritated Alastar beyond reason and he demanded that she *get lost.*

Alastar could feel his power slipping and it was very concerning to him. It bothered him so much that he no longer sat in the COD's nest anymore. He no longer wanted to even look at Bartus or that skinny snake, Devant. Somehow, everything was Devant's doing, and Alastar knew it. Bartus would have been far too stupid to engineer the situation so delicately. It hadn't escaped Alastar's notice that he was in the midst of a chess match.

Although Bartus's reputation was on the rise because of recent events, Alastar knew that he was more of a checkers guy, and not a great one at that. Alastar had to find a new place to brood. It turned out that there was an unused hallway in the basement of the library building. The place had been vacant for years. Alastar had pried away some boards to gain access to the space, and then a few more to give him a secret exit in case he ever needed to make a discreet tactical egress.

This time he didn't advertise his brooding location like he had with the COD's nest. All Alastar wanted at that point was to be alone with his thoughts. His thoughts, and his own damned frustration.

Devant.

If only he would die.

The problem was, that with the end of each passing day, Devant still lived — and his influence grew. The counselors had to be the key. Alastar had been watching them closely, and something deep inside his gut told him that the counselors would be the ones to expose Devant's Achilles' heel.

He closed his eyes, and he breathed. Then he willed himself to relax, to find his creative center. When his eyes opened, Alastar felt the anticipation of adventure. There was a cold thrill of danger, and the blind recklessness of intrigue. Alastar pulled a knife from the leather sheath on his belt, and touching his thumb to the edge, he frowned.

Could be sharper.

So Alastar pried his favorite stone from its place in the wall. This stone was his favorite because he often used it to sharpen things as he strategized. Alastar set to work on the blade in slow rhythmic strokes, and with each pull of the blade, Alastar imagined his enemies being cut low.

That evening, as the hours passed away, Alastar realized the crux of his problem. He himself needed to be sharpened, and Devant was the stone.

Every man needed sharpening, even Devant. That was why his counselors were there. Suddenly he could see it so clearly. It turned out that this was a very special game after all, an expert's game — and so far Alastar was losing.

The thoughts that were coming to him were finally beginning to make some sense, finally bringing him ideas that had substance, and the realization of it, brought him peace.

It had been so long.

Alastar closed his eyes and breathed deeply. And he breathed again. He could feel exhaustion wrapping its gentle arms around him, taking his thoughts on a meandering journey. Alastar let himself be taken, he let sleep come.

But it wasn't for long.

Quiet voices approaching from down his secret hallway roused him like cold water down his spine. Anger flared within him. He was just about to rise when he saw Sophia peek her small head into his darkened lair. This was his place, how could she think to intrude upon him as he rested?

He threw his knife at her as she was stepping through the broken boards that were the entryway of his private chamber. Sophia's eyes flared wide as she registered the flash of the blade but she managed to duck her head and collapse her body to the side, where she scrambled behind a pile of junk that was against the wall.

After a few moments she peeked out and Alastar launched his sharpening stone at her head. His aim was perfect and the stone shattered against the wall where Sophia's head had been just a moment before.

Then Sophia was on the move again. She closed the distance and was on Alastar less than a second later. She was literally, on Alastar. Sophia had wrapped herself around his waist. "Sleep." She said. "Go back to sleep." Her voice was small.

"Why did you come here?"

"It doesn't matter, I'm here now and the Keepers won't be kind if they catch us. So we're staying." She still hadn't eased up even a little on the Greco-Roman lock that she had around his waist.

"We?" Alastar said as he sat back, formally resigning himself to Sophia's bullying.

"Me and Demsie." She said. Sophia turned and called out in a hushed tone to encourage her friend to approach.

A weak voice sounded back from behind the broken boards. "But he's angry." The voice said.

"Not anymore. Come."

Time passed, and soon Alastar got tired of waiting. He closed his eyed and relaxed, letting himself pass into sleep once again, this time with Sophia's head pressed against his chest.

Soothing warmth.

Small voices, female sounds out of a far away place.

Over here, come. It's okay, he's asleep.

Footsteps approaching slowly.

But he throws things at you. Knives and stones.

Then Alastar felt another small body nestle in beside them both.

Yes, he does throw things at me. That was Sophia's voice. *But he always misses.*

I do.

THIRTEEN

Sophia's eyes snapped open at the sound of Demsie's agonized scream. Looking around, their barracks were undisturbed, and the other oracles were all where they should be. Unfortunately for Sophia, Demsie was not. Sophia's friend had crawled into bed with her in the middle of the night, which meant that when Demsie screamed, her mouth was positioned only a few inches from Sophia's ear. "Demsie, shush!"

Demsie's screaming went on.

Sophia grabbed her pillow and stuffed it over Demsie's face, muffling the sound just enough that the other oracles limited their complaints to acidic stares. It was several minutes before Demsie stopped screaming and then the girl began to shake.

Sophia's bed vibrated like it was coin operated. And she giggled at the sensation despite her friend's obvious distress. Then Sophia dug through the pillow, blankets, and the blond hair, until she could hold Demsie's pale pink cheeks in both her hands. "Demsie, what's wrong?"

Demsie didn't say a word but her lips moved like a fish sucking at algae. It made Sophia smile again. Demsie had always had a beautiful shape to her lips; they were her best feature. The other oracles were always jealous of her mouth, and often talked about it behind Demsie's back.

"Demsie." Sophia grabbed her friend's lips between her thumb and finger. "Focus!"

"My God, my God, the cod, the cod, it's odd, so odd, my God." Demsie's eyes opened and stared at Sophia but she knew that Demsie wasn't looking at her. She was seeing something else. Then she started to whimper loudly and Sophia had to put the pillow back over Demsie's face to avoid further irritating her roommates.

After several minutes, Sophia tried again. "Demsie, shush!"

But Demsie's fragile mind was beyond Sophia's reach. "Studor's balls!" Demsie screamed, and then she fell silent. The shaking had stopped as well. Two minutes later, Demsie was snoring.

Sophia stared at the ceiling, not even bothering to try and sleep. She was waiting for the sustained chime that would be directing the residents of her barracks to the shower hall. The bell rang within a few minutes, as Sophia knew that it would.

All of the girls sprung out of bed, pulled on pants, and then staggered out into the morning mists. They were as twitchy as a herd of frightened deer. There were no incidents on the way to the showers and no surprises in the shower building either. They cleaned up with military efficiency as they had since before they were old enough to remember.

As Sophia was pulling on her shirt, she noticed Demsie staring at her. "What?" Sophia said.

"Is he really the COD?"

Sophia looked into Demsie's eyes and her heart. She seemed lucid for the moment. She saw both her friend's urgency, and the underlying panic that was stirring her soul. Sophia kissed her friend on the cheek. "Demsie, be happy. We'll be all right today."

"No. Sophia tell me, is he really the COD?"

Why did she suddenly need to know? She had been muttering something about the cod in bed that morning. Sophia knew that Demsie was under tremendous stress, though. All the killers had been nosing around her since Alastar had left her undefended in the yard. The truth was, it would just be a matter of time before something horrible happened to her, but Sophia would never say that to her friend.

"I believe that he's the COD." Sophia said, as she tried to dismiss her own feelings that bad times were on the horizon. Some of the other oracles had begun staring at them both, and those girls were looking somewhat pale, and nauseous. The ones that weren't staring, were deliberately looking away, obviously trying to distract themselves from what they all knew.

"Okay." Demsie said. Then she turned and walked out of the change room.

Sophia felt completely alone.

The first day that Demsie had disappeared, almost nobody, other than Sophia, had cared enough to even discuss it. The next day though, speculation was rampant amongst the people who knew her.

After hours of listening to them go on and on about all of the painful possibilities for Demsie's sudden and unexplained disappearance, the group seemed to come to a consensus behind one particular theory. Of course that consensus had been reached without the hindrance of actual facts to confirm or deny their beliefs.

The theory was, that she had been taken by the Wandandan's. Even the idea of it made Sophia shiver. Everybody in the Station knew, that the Wandandans were a secret society. They operated under the shadows of night, and carried out all manner of atrocities, as they practiced dark ceremonies to honor their petty god Wandanda. It was a cult exclusive to the Station, and it was said to have existed for centuries, if that could be believed.

Even if they were measured in the category of *secret societies that everyone knows everything about*, the Wandandans would still be ranked somewhere just short of dead last. They had vague and fluctuating beliefs. They performed whichever random ceremonial acts they could scrounge up the resources for, and they had an uninspiring leader, whom everyone referred to as Witchy Wanda. Though her given Station name was Bett. Not even Betty.

The Wandandan's sacrificed whatever animals they could find, or even plants in a pinch because they were cultists that could not afford to be all that picky. It was said that at one point they used a bucket of earthworms to pay homage to their exceedingly undemanding god, because it was all anyone could find on short notice.

Bett, or Wanda, by her ceremonial title, was an oracle just a few years older than Sophia. The cult's tradition stated that the Wandandan leader had been transformed by divine action, from her mortal body into another body entirely androgynous by nature. It didn't seem plausible, since from what Sophia could tell, aside from the usual changes with puberty, Wanda had never experienced any transformation of note. In fact, the most androgynous thing about her was that she now cut her hair like a boy. Other evidence against her alleged sexual transformation was Wanda's dirty little habit of minxing around with any and all males that would have her.

Her followers did copious amounts of drugs, and were a general terror to the oracles. It was partly because they had a tendency to abduct female oracles for occasional use in their ceremonies, and partly because the oracles could sense the dark depths of unrighteousness that lurked inside Wandandan souls.

All the killers considered the Wandandans a farce and a joke, but the oracles knew better. It was true that as a cult, they were pathetic, but there was more to them than the killers knew. There was a reason why Studor allowed the Wandandans to exist. Studor had even taken it one step further. He made a fairly sizable concession to them by lodging all of the Wandandan oracles together, in order to keep them separate from the other oracles. If Studor hadn't agreed to that, the non-Wandandan oracles would have been having constant meltdowns in the Wandandan oracle's presence. Yuck, they were so filthy. For all of those reasons, Sophia had to conclude that Studor knew about the Wandandan's dreadful power.

Again she shivered. The thought of Demsie being used by the Wandandans was repulsive to her. She tried to force the thought from her mind. She knew that it was all just ridiculous conjecture anyways. There was no evidence, and if the Wandandans were to blame, there would be evidence. Everybody was always spying on the Wandandans, it was pretty much a Station's residents national pastime. Word of what the Wandandans were doing each night, spread through the pods like the daily news. It was the least secretive secret society in the history of all creation. If they had taken Demsie, it would've been all that anyone would have been talking about.

Sophia took a breath to try and clear her stress away. She knew that Alastar wouldn't help her, since he was busy practicing his cold blooded denial, telling himself that Demsie didn't mean any more to him than any other Station resident. The Station psychologists called it the *compartmentalizing of emotions*. Whatever the in term was, Sophia didn't approve. He could be so thick sometimes, that boy who never quite left her thoughts. Someday, she thought, he could grow into a good man.

CHAPTER FOURTEEN

FOURTEEN

Nobody had seen Demsie for three days and from what Alastar could see, all Sophia ever did anymore was cry. She had cried all through their decryption class and their applied toxicology class. Her eyes were constantly red and swollen. It was like she had been infected with something.

Alastar knew that he wanted nothing to do with her in her current state. Her unhappiness made him feel awkward. Josh seemed to be intrigued by it though. He spent his time hovering around her, which was fine. Maybe Josh could somehow make her dry up. Alastar knew that he was too busy for all of that drama anyways.

He had been spending his time doing reconnaissance on Devant's counselors. Now he knew their basic habits, their individual duties, where they ate lunch, and most importantly, when they were going to sneak Devant off to the Burrow.

He had learned a bit about Devant too, like how he killed without anyone seeing him come into contact with the victim. He was using a fine string, barely visible, perhaps a single strand of silk, with a tiny weighted barb attached to the tip. Alastar was certain that the ingeniously subtle weapon was what the counselors had referred to as Mosquito. A potent poison on the tip of the barb would be all that would be needed to put one's enemies to sleep with no more force than a whisper.

Tonight Alastar planned to tag along and see what he could learn from Devant's counseling session.

Alastar stepped out of his barracks. He was changed and ready for Human Powered Weapon's practice. It was an interesting course involving every type of steel, wood, or bone weapon ever invented from the dawn of time until now. Most of it was pretty archaic stuff and the other resident's complained out loud about having to learn it, but not Alastar. He was always the dominant force in the room whenever it came time to get medieval on each other.

When he stepped out of his doorway, Desda saw him from the corner of her eye and spun towards him with a huge smile. Her shining hair flared out into the air like a fan and then snapped back with a bounce, letting the loose brown curls settle to frame her near perfect face. She gave a delicate wave to him by raising her hand just a bit, and then paused as though remembering something. After that she walked over to him.

"Meet me after sessions today? I've got something that I want to um, share with you."

Her eyes were expectant and seemed maybe a little bit worried that he might say no. "Okay." Alastar said.

She breathed a sigh of relief, which caused Alastar to smile at her.

"I'll be behind the gallows by the little kid's dungeon and we can go from there. At seventeen hundred hours, okay?"

"Confirmed." Alastar said.

Alastar watched her walk away. She looked back and saw him watching, and she smiled at him again.

That day Alastar reveled in the pummeling of his opponents right up until the final minutes of his session. The African knobkerrie that he held, was feeling as at home in his hand, as it ever had in a Zulu warrior's. Alastar laid the knobkerrie's hardwood nodule to head, knee and spine with a sportsman's speed and an artist's grace. If his opponents hadn't been thoroughly armored, they wouldn't have ever left the room. By the time the session was done, he felt exhilarated, and ready to see what Desda had in store for him.

He found himself feeling a bit reminiscent as he walked the thin trail towards the little kid's dungeon. It made him think of Studor and all the times that the two of them had matched wits in the past. Studor was smart. Really smart, and he symbolized the power that Alastar planned to achieve someday, once his body was full grown and his education was complete.

The gallows were just up ahead so Alastar left the trail in order to sweep the area. Just a precaution, but one never could be too sure. He moved through the wooded area like a ghost, silent and swift. He paused to listen every once in a while, but heard only the reassuring chatter of birds in the high trees. Alastar was checking the best ambush sites, as Desda wandered into the clearing behind the gallows. She was leaning casually on a stump when Alastar emerged from the trees.

She smiled. "Come." She said as she took his hand to lead him away, across the clearing.

Alastar let himself be led. She smiled back at him brightly as they plunged into the woods. There was no trail that he could see. The ground that they followed seemed to rise as they were going north and somewhat west. "It's up ahead." She said. "I found it during an assignment. It seems almost ancient, and you'll never believe what's in it."

"Have you shown anyone else?" Alastar said.

For a while Desda said nothing, then she smiled back at him. "Of course not. I want you to be my first."

They were almost forty minutes out from where they had begun before Desda stopped.

"We're here." She said.

Alastar looked around. "There's nothing here."

"Yes." Desda said as she pulled a tarp aside that was covered with dirt and small weeds. "There is."

Beneath the tarp was a stone slab, carved with runes. The stone itself looked ancient, but Alastar couldn't quite recognize the culture. Perhaps Phoenician.

"Help me lift the slab." Desda said. It took all of their combined strength to slide the slab sideways enough for them to fit their bodies into the gap below. "Come'on. I want to show you what's below."

Desda slipped her body into the opening and disappeared beneath the earth. Alastar followed.

There was a sort of stairs cut into the ground, covered by stones which had long since settled into a disorganized chaos that would no doubt have made the stairway's architect lose heart.

They followed the tunnel down into the earth and Desda pulled out a small flashlight. The walls were carved, not natural, and they had wooden beams to support them. The air in this place seemed uncommonly dry, with no smell of rot or any kind of musty odor. Alastar wondered a little about the stability of the passageway, but Desda continued to pull him forward. Although he would have been sorely disappointed if he were buried alive, he was willing to take the chance that it wouldn't happen.

The hallway widened out and became more decorative, with purely aesthetic columns and carvings on the walls. All of it looked ancient.

They walked past some statues. Two nude men locked into battle like Cain and Able, an innocent looking woman in her natural state, a powerful demigod with the body of a dragon and a smile like laughing Buddha. As well as others that were more difficult to define.

Why was this place here? It had nothing to do with Station training.

Could Studor actually be ignorant to the presence of an archaeological treasure trove located right on his own grounds?

Alastar stopped in his tracks and grabbed Desda. "Wait." He said. "Studor may have laid traps."

"I've been up and down this hall a few times. If there were traps I would have tripped them already. C'mon, it's just up ahead."

There were corridors branching right and left from the main passage that Desda was leading him down. Alastar could see by the dust on the floor and the cobwebs that these tunnels had not seen much use of late. He wondered how far the tunnels might go. It might have even been possible that the caverns could lead him to a place outside of Station grounds. How many years of exploration would it take to find out?

The passage ended abruptly in a wide rectangular room. There was a massive slab of stone, triangular in shape that covered the floor. It had similar runes on it as the stone that Desda and him had slid aside at the entrance to the cavern. It made Alastar wonder if this huge slab could be a door of some sort. As he looked around the room, he noted stone chairs, a table, some shelves carved into the wall holding hundreds of trinkets and items. Underneath a stone arch and recessed into the shadows was a huge stone door, it looked like some ancient vault out of Mesopotamia. If it was, then the giant serpent that wound its body around the outside of the door would be the god Tiamat, or as modern people knew him, Leviathan.

Alastar took in the whole room. It was quite a treasure that Desda was sharing with him. He looked over at her and nodded his approval.

She smiled. "That's not all." Desda skipped over to the shelves and pulled out a dust covered glass bottle. It looked like an old wine bottle. Not ancient, but old. She placed the bottle in his hands. The label was in French and was peeling at the edges.

"Seventeen eighty-nine Chateau d'Yquem." Alastar said. "Impressive."

"I know, right? I did some research, seventeen eighty-seven was a better year but still, isn't this exciting?"

Alastar rubbed some dust away from the label. "Seventeen eighty-nine is still an excellent bottle of wine, Desda. The Suavage family and the Lur-Saluces of Chateau de Fargues were still combining their efforts at that time. The value of the seventeen eighty-seven is largely due to the influence of some elites in popular culture and microeconomics, rather than any vast differences in the quality."

Desda looked at him expressionless. "How do you know all that? I mean, I know it 'cause I just researched it, but how do you know it?"

Alastar smiled at her. "Don't you think I read, Desda? We were learning about wines and liquor's influences on culture and economics when we were still seveners."

"You remember that stuff?" She said with a look of respect in her eyes that nearly bordered on fear.

He kept his smile wide to put her at ease again. "I don't miss much, Desda."

Desda swallowed and said nothing. Then she turned away.

Alastar was wondering what was up with her, but then she turned around, eyes sparkling once again and said. "Shall we drink it?"

She stepped towards him and wrapped an arm around his waist while pulling her body against his, and then she bent down and kissed him on the lips.

Pulling away, Desda took the bottle from his hands and danced towards the shelves again, where two ceramic cups were resting. Alastar watched as she used a tool to work the cap free and then she set the bottle on the shelf to give the wine a chance to breath.

Desda brought Alastar the cork to let him smell it. The wine seemed good. Alastar pretty much expected vinegar when he was first offered to sniff the cap. She laughed when she saw that Alastar approved, then Desda grabbed his hand and pulled him over to a wide stone chair. It looked almost like a throne, and it was much too big for him. "Sit here and I'll serve you." Then Desda danced away again.

She stood at the shelf and tinkered with the drinks as Alastar surveyed the room. It was dark where Alastar was because Desda had the flashlight, but he saw some torches ensconced on the wall. He walked over to a torch and pulled it free. Then he smelled it. It still seemed to have fuel on it, which was surprising, so he pulled out a match and lit it.

The dark corners of the room receded, retreating before the flashing firelight. More shelves with more books, bottles, and trinkets lined the walls. He placed the torch in its holder and returned to sit on his throne.

Desda brought the wine to him and handed him a cup. "Taste it." She said.

Alastar smelled the wine as he swirled it against the edges of his glass, then he poured just a hint onto his tongue, letting the various tastes reveal themselves. It was wonderfully complex, except for the somewhat savory after taste, which Alastar assumed was a result of the age of this particular bottle.

Desda drank and giggled. "My first Chateau d'Yquem." Then she paused and looked long at Alastar. "Do you think I'm pretty?"

Of course he did. "Yes."

Desda gave a sigh of relief and looked down at her wine. "Good." She said.

He sipped his wine again and they looked at each other in the flickering torchlight. Then she leaned towards him and kissed him again. "When you're a little older you'll want to do more than kiss me."

"Maybe." Alastar said.

"Can I tell you a secret?" Desda said.

"Okay."

She sipped at her wine and smiled playfully. "This wine is making my head feel a bit funny. How much alcohol do you think is in it?"

"Some. I feel it too." He said. "What's your secret?"

"I thought that I was in love once." She stared at him hard. "I really did. I mean, I know that I'm a psychopath, right? And you and I know that love doesn't come easily for us, but for a while I thought that I might be different. I just thought." She fell silent.

"What happened?"

Desda was slow to answer. "He died. And then I got over it, and I knew it couldn't have been love. But for months I wondered. I wondered if we had been given more time together, if maybe it could have turned into love. Is that crazy?"

"It's not crazy." Alastar sipped his wine. "How did he die?"

"A mine field. He was blown up."

Alastar remembered the day. A lot of twelvers died that morning. "I'm sorry. I'm sure he was an able combatant."

Desda smiled. "Not as able as you." She drank some wine.

They sat together on the throne until their cups were drained and then Desda got up to pour them each another glass.

The alcohol felt strange in Alastar's body. He seemed relaxed and invigorated all at the same time. It was a good feeling, but powerful. "Just one more glass." He told her.

She returned to the throne and sat beside him, leaning her body into his. "Now you tell me a secret. I told you one and fair is fair."

"What type of secret would I tell you? Are you looking for the secret to my strength, like the one Samson gave to Delilah?"

Desda laughed. "No, nothing so dangerous. That type of knowledge could get me killed. Tell me something that others don't know about the legend of Alastar Daivi. Let me think. What did you say that Smacks wanted to know? I remember now — Tell me where you were when you missed all your sessions a while back? I know that you're not telling everyone just because they're all so desperate to know, and you're too stubborn." Desda laughed. "Tell me that and we'll be even."

Desda bent to kiss him again. Her lips felt soft against his skin, and this time he tried to kiss her back, but she pulled away before he could. Alastar looked into her eyes and found himself deeply satisfied with this moment. The place, the wine, and the company all felt so comfortable, he would have loved to stay there forever.

She leaned towards his ear and gave it a little nibble with her lips. He laughed it felt so good. "Tell me." She whispered in a tone that imitated a threat.

"Okay, but I can only tell you what I know."

"Alright." She said.

"Nothing. I know nothing about what happened. Any memories I have, are gone completely."

Desda's mouth hung limp for just a moment, then she laughed. "No you're not getting off that easy!" She stood up from where she perched on the throne and positioned herself in front of him. "Fair is fair. I told you a secret that would make me look weak in the eyes of the other killers, and you think you can get off by just saying that you forgot?" She moved her lips close to his but didn't kiss him.

"I didn't forget. I'm not sure I ever knew. For all I know I was unconscious for the entire time. I would tell you if I could. It's stupid that everyone wants to know about that week, even though I've never ever claimed that I knew what happened to me. It's just a blank spot in my memory, not a part of the Alastar Daivi legend at all."

Desda looked at him, seeming confused and somewhat hurt. "I thought we knew each other better." Her voice was tinged with anger. She walked away and stood in the shadows on the far side of the room. Then she moaned and slumped to the floor.

Alastar rushed to her side, aware of the alcohol's effect on his coordination and balance. Suddenly, from out of the darkness of an adjoining passage, Smacks and three others fell upon him, taking him quickly to the floor with their superior masses.

Desda lifted her head and looked over at him. "Alastar!" She cried, the concern evident in her voice.

"Shut up bitch." Frizz growled as he backhanded her across the cheek.

They must have done something to her so she wasn't able to fight back though. Alastar strained to break free, but it was no use. He was captured. How did they find him? He knew that they must have followed him there. Smacks had probably been planning this day for a long time.

Alastar soon found himself lashed to the chair by thin weaves of metallic cord. The kind of stuff that was light to carry, but had enough tensile strength to restrain a bull elephant. Meanwhile Desda was dragged, screaming into the darkness of an adjoining hallway.

Then Smacks was in his face and Alastar saw up close the ugly imperfection that had once been Smacks' perfect nose, before a certain wooden club had been redirected and scarred it up. "You know what I want, Daivi! And to think that I almost got it for free, just because you wanted to bone that stupid bitch. Tell me or your girlfriend suffers. You're going to tell me in the end anyways, why not save us all the trouble?"

Alastar wished that his thoughts weren't so cloudy. If his head were clear maybe he could manage the situation. His thoughts were swimming with useless ideas. *Smacks is probably right, in the end I'll have to comply.*

"Why lose Desda? Isn't she about the only ally that you have anymore? The only one that isn't a scrawny oracle who cries more than she kisses." Smacks turned and yelled. "Frizz, make her wail."

Sounds issued forth from the darkened hall. He had never heard Desda sound so desperate. "Stop!" Alastar screamed. "I don't know, I don't know. You heard me tell her that I don't know."

Smacks hammered a fist into Alastar's midsection. "Make her hurt, Frizz." Smacks said.

The sounds of Desda's misery echoed once again through the caverns and Alastar spurred himself to think of a strategy. His brain was like quicksand though, conceiving only the simplest thoughts. Think. Think. Alastar breathed deeply. A lie! He needed to lie.

Alastar tried to compose a fabricated tale of what might have kept him busy for the week in the Burrow, but this strange state of drunkenness —

No. It was more than drunkenness; there were other chemicals at play here.

Station youth were often drugged during all manner of exercises. Alastar knew what drunk felt like and —"

Desda's scream shook Alastar back to the task at hand. The lie, he needed to work on the lie.

"Tell me." Smacks breath was hot in his face. "You know that you'll have to tell me anyways."

"Okay." Alastar said even before he had thought about what he was saying. "I'll tell"

The lie! It's not ready.

"I was on a special assignment. An old fat man." *Studor's balls, that was too much of the truth!* It wasn't even remotely the lie that Alastar had been preparing. "He had a beard."

Smacks looked at him, his strong features were stony as he appraised what Alastar was telling him. "What did the bearded man want? What was the op?"

"I killed a man!" Alastar blurted. But in the lie Alastar had been forming, it was supposed to be a girl. "A girl, I mean a girl."

Smacks raised an eyebrow at Alastar. *Shit.* "A man, it was a man, but he was a cross-dresser. Some sick shit he was into, let me tell you."

Smacks' disbelief flickered into interest. Seeding a story with atypical details always made a lie more believable. Alastar decided to go with that. "He was an Asian guy that could work a short skirt like a Rockette, but Rockette's aren't Asian, so this guy needed killing and I ended him."

Alastar found himself babbling like a brook because of the poison shit that was in his blood stream. It made him want to just keep on talking. He had to pull himself together.

"How'd you do it?"

"Poison." *Shit*! That wasn't the lie either. He should have never let himself think of poison. "Poison bullet."

Smacks drilled his fist into Alastar's chin. "Do I look like an idiot? Who poisons a bullet? Besides why would they want you to run the op, you're a snot nosed kid."

It wasn't snot running from Alastar's nose it was blood. "I could use a Kleenex, please." Alastar said absent-mindedly and got drilled again for the comment.

Meanwhile Desda was screaming from the darkness.

"Talk!" Smacks screamed at him more than a little of Smacks' saliva hitting Alastar in the face.

"It's true!" Alastar screamed. "I used a poison bullet!" Station residents were taught never to retract any part of a lie if they were hoping to be believed. You had to fabricate your way forward to a more believable story whenever you encountered doubt. Never back off a lie. "It was a pellet gun. I poisoned a pellet and I shot him like I was just some kid playing a prank. Guy chased me for a bit and then gave up to go get a tissue so that the blood didn't stain his collar. Two days later, the guy died in his sleep and the fat man let me come back to the Station. That's it, I swear."

Desda's screaming stopped.

Smacks studied Alastar. His expression suggested that he still partly doubted Alastar's story but was also partly moved by respect. Smacks gang of thugs stopped what they were doing and gathered round, believing that the interrogation had run its course.

Then it was Alastar's turn to be surprised. Desda, looking beautiful as always, strolled out of the darkness with a smug look of satisfaction on her face. She was unharmed.

She approached Alastar, who was still tied to his chair. Then she balled up her fist and she struck him. "You killed him, you little shit. You killed them all. All the twelvers just so you could build your precious legend. You always walk around so arrogant, but now you're gonna die. Oh, and by the way, kissing you makes me vomit." Then she scratched Alastar's face with her claws, leaving streaks of blood. "I loved him you asshole. Of course I loved him."

Alastar's drug addled brain was slowly putting the pieces together. Of course she was betraying him. The signs were all there. The fear, the withdrawn behaviors, the sexual manipulation, but the surest sign should have been the stone at the entrance to the tunnels. It was far too heavy for her to have ever moved by herself.

She was a liar. And Alastar was a sucker. Sadly, soon he would be a dead sucker. They thought they had what they wanted, so the only thing left for them to do was kill him.

Alastar focused his attention on Smacks. He stared deep into the man's hard eyes, and without a single flicker of any muscle on his face; Alastar let the killer see a momentary flash of mischief in his eyes. Then he looked away as though he were trying to hide it.

Desda was still reveling in her revenge, acting as though she had won this victory single handedly, so Alastar decided to use her arrogance to his advantage.

Although Alastar's thoughts were still muddled, he had the presence of mind to remember who his opponent was.

Smacks loves Smacks like Tracker is dead. It was the new saying ever since Tracker had met his demise in the woods, the day that Smacks' nose had become imperfect. He needed to use the killer's arrogance, so Alastar pulled together his best lie and addressed Desda. "So you managed to manipulate me and your lackeys so that you could get what you wanted. But I saw you with the fat man, Desda. You didn't fool me for a second. Only an idiot would have believed that you could slide away the stone and get in to explore this passage by yourself. The only thing that surprised me was that you could get Smacks eating out of your hand the way that he is now. You won't ever know the full story, so you can tell the fat man that whatever he's giving you for this, it's going to be too much."

Desda looked at Alastar, wondering. Then Desda looked at Smacks. Smacks tightened his lips and said to her. "Five seconds. I give you five seconds.

"He's lying! Of course he's lying. Why would you believe him?" Desda's long lashes flickered frantically like a startled hummingbird's wings.

Smacks smiled at her. "I don't really. I know he's lying about something. But you know, that last thing that he said seemed pretty convincing. And with all of that Sugar and Synthamphetamines in his system, I've got a tendency to believe what he's saying." Smacks turned his sizable shoulders to face Desda square on. "Mostly though, I don't like your cocky attitude with all your *I loved him and now you're gonna taste my revenge,* crap. Besides, who told you to come out of the hallway anyways, we weren't finished the interrogation yet."

"Smacks, you know I never said that." Desda's eyes were big. She was backing away, but Frizz was right behind her. "I thought you got what you wanted, so I came out."

Alastar knew that her pleading was useless. The truth was, Alastar had cast doubts upon her loyalty. That and her current utter lack of usefulness would be more than enough for the circumstantial evidence to be convict by this court.

"Can I do it?" Frizz asked politely.

"Soon." Smacks said. "Tie her up for now. And give them both a shot of the truth cocktail. I want them swimming in confusion before we get back to business.

Alastar knew that he was in a tight spot. But truthfully, Alastar felt pretty good about the short term outcome. He had divided their alliance, if only somewhat, and he had made Smacks believe that Alastar still had some knowledge that needed to be extracted. What troubled Alastar, was that he couldn't conceive of any way that he could come out of this situation alive. With yet another shot of drugs in his system it was unlikely that he would ever be able to think up a decent plan.

The truth was, Alastar needed outside help, which would never come. Sophia might be the only one to care about him any more, since his allies had distanced themselves. And she would be too preoccupied with crying over Demsie's disappearance. Would Sophia somehow sense his need, even through her grief? Not that it would matter if she did. Even though oracles could turn up at the least likely times, any oracle coming to rescue him from this group of killers would have to be on a suicide mission. He should have never been so stubborn with Josh and the boys, those guys would have come in handy right about now.

Alastar focused on the tactical problem at hand. He had four enemies, assuming that Desda stayed tied up. He knew that Smacks was an egomaniac and that Frizz was a sadistic moron. Smacks two other minions meant nothing to him, they were just muscle as far as Alastar could see.

For the time being, Smacks had retired to the corner of the room where he was inspecting the shelves and their contents. There was a play there but Alastar's muddled brain couldn't see it. Before long, a needle was plunged into Alastar's brachial artery and he still hadn't come up with any sort of plan.

The minion whose ears were bent over like little awnings pressed the plunger, and the drugs hit Alastar's brain with a rush.

CHAPTER FIFTEEN

FIFTEEN

Cold ground.

It had worn her fingers to bloody stubs, and she felt only numbness as she continued to claw her way towards the living. Oracles weren't built to suffer this much. They were not well suited to spend days under the earth. Entombed and isolated. There were ancient ones there who were fighting to drive her back.

She had to claw.

The air was thick, and she cried to herself as she struggled. Far away she could sense Sophia's fear for her. Sophia would know that she was alive, but it would be causing her so much pain. Most people, including the other oracles thought that Demsie was crazy, and perhaps she was, but that didn't mean that she was wrong.

She clawed at the dark dirt.

They kept yelling at her and trying to confuse her, but they weren't touching her. They couldn't, she was under shelter. But they were horrible, and they upset her. They told her she was going to die without water. It was true, but then why were they scared? Why did they care about a young girl buried under the earth?

Demsie pulled at a root. This deep? There had been so many roots two days before, but she hadn't seen them much since that long ago. That was when the coyotes had wanted to nip at her, but they quickly learned better. There had been a battle, and they had drawn each other's blood and then a respect formed between them. She didn't fault the creatures; they were only defending their home.

She cut at the root with her knife. Why did she have so many enemies? The question hung in her mind like a balloon on a windless day. She knew about joy, and she knew about peace. The other residents didn't, even Sophia.

For all of the ways that Sophia was wondrous, she didn't see those things. She didn't see the purity or the, ouch! They were screaming in her head. Ow, ow, ow, oh God please stop them.

Silence.

She didn't see any of that, but Demsie knew what she saw. Demsie had never been as smart, or as capable, or as pretty, and the other oracles had always had to hold onto Demsie's hand so that she didn't wander off. Demsie could get confused so easily, by the things that sprang from the eyes and ears of her heart.

And Sophia had Alastar. Demsie felt jealousy creep into her heart. A type of it anyway. Nobody really had Alastar. He had let Charlie piss on her. The humiliation was still fresh and Demsie had to stop crawling for a while. She sobbed out loud.

They all started laughing at her and mocking her. She hated them. They were dark like the tomb that she was mucking through, mucking to, mucka mucka mucka do.

She hummed that to herself as she clawed forward. The air was so thick, she had breathed the same molecules about a thousand times already. Why was she still alive?

Alastar's world was a mix of pain and confusion. Smacks had been thorough in his interrogation and Alastar had said a lot. He had told lies, and he had told truth. He had embellished on details, and kept his mouth defiantly shut about matters which he knew nothing about anyways. Of course the more Alastar said, or did not say, the more Smacks believed that the Legend was holding out on him.

"Dammit Legend! You're as slippery as a whore's thighs. It's going to be a shame to put you down. You should have accepted my offer of friendship."

"I did dammitz." Alastar had been slurring his words since Smacks' minions had dosed him again. "I shaid we wuz friendsz."

Smacks looked at the younger killer and smiled. "Yeah you did, but you didn't really mean it, did you?"

Alastar shrugged. The gesture lanced pain through his bruised and broken up ribs. "I guess notsz."

"Yes Legend, honesty is always the best policy."

"Indeedsz." Alastar slurred, which made Smacks laugh out loud. "Sho it sheemsz we are it an impassz. I shuggest a trucshe."

"A truce you say? Isn't that rich. And what do I get out of this truce,

Legend?"

Alastar smiled a bloody smile. "Appre-ciationsz."

Smacks beamed at Alastar. He really did have a charming smile. "I wish I could Legend. I truly wish I could."

Then Smacks drilled Alastar in the throat.

Demsie pressed her bloody fingers into the cold earth that was in front of her and she felt the dirt fall away.

An air pocket.

She had encountered them before. It would likely be some moles doing, no doubt.

She plunged her hand through. It went in easily. Demsie put her other hand to the task as well. The air pocket seemed big. Bigger than a mole's tunnel. Could it be another coyote den? She hoped not. She had no energy to fight anymore.

Demsie pushed herself forward with her legs and squeezed herself through the gap into the open space. It felt like being born.

Some are born of blood, some are born of water, and others are born of earth. Demsie broke through into the dry air beyond, whimpered, and then cried just as she had on her very first day. Only this day there were no loving hands to catch her up and clean her bloodied flesh.

Demsie lay in the darkness weeping softly, breathing the clean dry air, as she tried to block out all the voices that were condemning her for living through her second birth.

Alastar's head fell sluggishly to the side. It caused pain to lance throughout his neck, all the way to his jaw, jolting him upright with a start. He looked around. Where was Smacks?

Alastar looked over at Desda. It took him a while to decide, but eventually he resolved that she was dead. He hadn't noticed them killing her.

Desda. She had been really good looking.

Frizz walked by. He went right through the room, without even looking at Alastar. Where was Smacks?

Alastar pulled at his bonds. It only served to irritate his raw wrists, so he gave up after a couple of minutes. Alastar looked around. Where was Smacks?

His head was so foggy, but somehow he needed to kill Smacks.

It would never happen. He knew it. Never.

He heard Smacks' voice filtering from down a darkened hall of the cavern. Maybe it had always been there, the sound wasn't even all that faint. Alastar desperately wished that he had his perception working the way it should have. His eyes seemed too blurred. The taste of metal was in his mouth. His ears were ringing, and his lips felt fat as sausage.

Alastar looked around the room. Desda seemed dead. Where was Smacks?

The old ones were horrible in this cavern, jammed in thick like the rock and mud that separated her from the light above. They had teased her ruthlessly as she gathered her supplies, but Demsie kept her hands busy. *Sophia had said that he was the COD*, she told herself.

She knew what had to happen next, just like she had known that she had to fight her way into that coyote den to start her tunnel. But back then, she had a sharpened stick to help her. Now she only had a survival knife, a cloth, a plastic vial of high-octane fuel, and some chloroform. Not exactly an arsenal.

The old ones were laughing. She hated them. *Where was the bright one*?

Oh. Up ahead.

But what if he wasn't real? The doctors had told her not to always trust everything she saw. They said that because of her psychosis, her subconscious might manufacture more favorable realities for her to interact with. Creating false allies and opportunities. They seemed to believe that the bright one was a product of what they called, *her idealistic yearnings for a champion or savior*, and they advised her to *stop all interaction with the bright one at once.*

Her doctor had thumped his desk hard when he had said it. She had never seen that doctor thump the desk before, and she had known him for as long as she could remember.

She looked in the direction where the bright one was. There was nobody there now. Demsie wondered for a while, *had he even been there?* Then she followed.

Her calf screamed with each step where the coyote had been biting her. She shuddered at the memory of the choked growl in the coyote's throat as that bitch's teeth had pulled at her flesh. It was a horrible sound and it made her feel sick. Almost as sick as she had felt when she plunged her sharpened stick into that coyote's soft fleshy torso. The bitch had yelped and run away.

The pain in Demsie's ankle made her remember, but she could still limp forward with it, so she would.

It was very dark, but she didn't dare unshutter her little light. Instead she did the opposite, only flashing it on momentarily every once in a while so she could memorize the caverns dimensions and check for hazards. Then she would proceed forward in the dark, going by feel. The old ones had been trying to deceive her, but she was still able to go forward.

So many turns, and so much darkness. Just like a pit of hell, this place felt like death to her. Time passed slowly in the black, as she wandered the twisted catacombs. Then, like the buzz of a distant fly in her ear came the sound of the first human voices that she had heard in days.

Demsie heard the voices, and she knew they meant danger to her, but she still walked towards them. The voices were superior to her, in both strength and number, and still she went forward. The words that those voices used were the icy cold thoughts of seasoned killers, made manifest. Yet she would not turn back.

He is the COD. Sophia had told her that she thought he was the COD.

Soon she was close enough to listen easily, and Demsie could recognize Smacks' voice. Of the killers, he would be the one to hurt her.

Demsie reached into her pocket and pulled out her rag and her chloroform. For it to work, she would have to get them to breath it. But how could she do that without them catching her?

Demsie stared down at her silly tools through the filtered light that was reflecting towards her, from the killer's lamps. It wasn't enough. She wasn't enough. And Smacks was going to hurt her terribly.

That thought made her clutch at her knife defensively and take a few steps backward, into the darkness.

No. He was the COD.

She had to do something. She stared at her knife as though the cold steel would somehow grow into an enchanted blade, one suitable for a he-to knight to wield into battle. She was not enough though.

Alastar would have been enough. *What would he do if it were me that was held captive?*

As soon as she thought that thought, the old ones began laughing at her. *Leave you! Leave you! Leave you to die!*

The words rang true and stung at her soul. So much so that Demsie felt her throat tighten as she stifled a sob. Then a cold sweat broke out on her neck as soon as she had made the soft strangled noise. Would they hear it?

Demsie listened.

The killers seemed silent. And the old ones laughed and laughed.

Demsie's feet padded silently away from the killers as fast as she could go safely. Then there was a sound.

"What was that?" One killer said.

"An animal?"

"Could be. Check it out."

Demsie's spine tingled in fear and her feet became glued to the rock where she stood. She was going to die there, almost certainly.

Demsie pressed herself into a cleft in the rock and willed herself to keep from crying out, so that she wouldn't give away her position. Then her hand touched something metallic which startled her.

Demsie wanted to run, but she didn't dare.

The old ones had begun speaking in whispers, their voices unintelligible. It sounded like some cryptic proto-Latin dialect and it made her want to scream. She felt the energy building in her throat, the scream was definitely coming.

Stop Demsie! Studor's balls, who just said that?

Demsie's gaze shot up and down the corridor, searching. There was nobody. *Calm, sweetheart.*

Demsie's eyes welled up in tears, which blurred her vision. She loved that voice. She loved it. Wiping the tears away and tasting their salt on her smile, Demsie breathed deeply, and could almost smell Sophia's hair. So dark and beautiful.

Forget about Alastar! He was the wrong example. What would Sophia do?

She would do what was needed, and she would use whatever she had to get it done.

Demsie reached for the metal that she had felt in the crevasse of the rock. This metal would be her friend. *Hello metal.* Demsie smiled as she grabbed her knife and began twisting the cap off the hollow handle.

Every survival knife had a hollow handle stuffed with compact tools.

The casual scuffing of heavy feet sounded the approach of one lone killer, making his way towards her. It was too dark to see, but she dumped the contents of the handle into her palm. The inside of the cap felt like the smooth rounded surface of a compass. No help there.

Matches. Tinder. Snare wire. No! Not snare wire, trip wire.

Demsie's hands worked fast. She had always had fast hands. She attached the slim wire to the metal, twisting it several times, praying that it would be enough to hold. Then she scurried to the far side of the corridor and pressed herself into a similar cleft in the rock on the other side of the hall. Demsie made herself very small, holding her tiny roll of trip cord ready in one hand and in the other hand, the cold steel knife.

The steps came closer, but the killer seemed to be in no hurry. Realizing that she had the time, Demsie set her hands to work on the chloroform bottle, dumping the anaesthetic onto the cloth, and holding her breath as the killer's light approached.

Demsie pressed deeper into her crevasse and thanked God that she was small. She held her wire slack, believing that it would be harder for the killer to see if it were along the ground. Demsie's heart thumped hard inside her chest as the killer stepped into view, and for a moment she feared that he could hear it. Although she was still holding her breath, the chloroform in the air tickled at her nose, and Demsie prayed that the killer wouldn't smell it.

When the killer's light fell upon her, Demsie almost screamed. First she felt shock, and then she felt panic. Demsie was certain that she would be discovered, but when the light slipped casually off of her, leaving her in darkness, she realized something. The days that Demsie had spent underground, digging her way into this horrible place, had left her looking much more like a very big lump of dirt than a very small human.

Demsie held her wire ready, and focused on the rhythm of the killer's plodding feet. Closer, closer, closer. When the killer's foot struck the right patch of dirt, she pulled the wire tight.

Demsie felt the wire jerk, when the killer's boot caught it. She pulled back with every bit of her strength, and then she watched as the killer grasped at empty air, trying to keep his balance. His body was tipping and his weight pulled forward, while his foot strained at the thin piece of wire.

For a moment Demsie wondered if this might be the dumbest thing that she had ever done. She didn't wonder long though because in the next moment, she felt herself getting physically jerked forward by the wire, as the killer crashed hard onto the floor of the cavern.

Demsie squealed as she clung desperately to her precious metallic thread and got thrown into the center of the hall. Quite suddenly, she found herself nearly nose to nose with her adversary. There was rancid breath hot on her face, assaulting her senses.

She squealed again.

The killer smiled. "Hello sweetheart." He whispered. "Give us a kiss?"

There was so much cruelty and death in this one. So much darkness that Demsie screamed with every bit of strength in her soul.

Even as the killer pressed his lips towards her, she pushed his face away with her small hands. The killer laughed and grasped at her shirt so that she couldn't escape.

It was a game to him.

Demsie pushed and pushed as the killer pulled at her, forcing his lips closer to Demsie's face. She fought him relentlessly, even though he seemed so strong! And then suddenly, he wasn't.

His grasp got clumsy and weak, and his shadowy eyes seemed to lose their carnal focus on her.

Demsie shoved his massive head away from her and the killer rolled onto his back with all the compliance of a limp noodle. Demsie shot to her feet, still wondering what had happened. Then she looked down at her hand. The chloroform soaked rag was still there.

The anesthetic cloth had been smeared with dirt, but it was still wet with the drug.

Demsie's knees gave way and she slumped to the ground as her brain slowly pieced together what had just happened. The cloth had been in her hand when she was pushing the killer's face away. She had won, but it was a complete fluke. Demsie choked back a wave of nausea and began to shake.

She should never have come. She was nowhere near capable enough for this task and she knew it.

Then the killer moaned. His fat hand reached up and fumbled at his face and lips. Demsie's heart doubled its pace.

"No!" She said as she tore the stopper off the chloroform bottle and dumped the contents clumsily onto the killer's face, his shirt, and into his mouth. Then she kicked him in the ribs for no reason but hatred, unfortunately hurting her toe in the process. The killer didn't stir.

Her mind was still racing as a type of paralysis came over her. She stared at the now useless, empty chloroform bottle that she held in her hand. What if he came awake again? Suddenly Demsie thought of her survival knife, it's cold steel beckoned to her with the promise of safety, and peace. She pulled out the blade.

Do it! Do it! The old ones screamed at her. Filthy.

A new wave of nausea struck her as she realized their perversion and Demsie dropped the blade onto the floor of the cavern.

Footsteps! They were running towards her.

Demsie scurried sideways like a startled animal and tucked herself into her tiny crevasse, where she hid in the darkness, shaking violently.

Demsie stuffed her hands into her pockets, looking for a weapon that her rational mind knew would not be there. The killer's came quickly.

Seeing their fallen ally, they stopped short and readied their weapons. Both of them held long blades forged of wicked black metal. The blades were almost invisible in the darkness of the cave. One of the killers held a torch high and in front of him. They studied the area, looking for any sign of ambush.

Demsie froze.

One of them muttered the word *chloroform*, but Demsie couldn't tell which.

The leader's eyes stopped. He was looking right at her. He pointed to where she hid in the darkened crevasse. Nodding agreement, the two men approached together.

They would only see a dirt lump. She was just a lump! No. They were coming for her. Step by step they grew closer. She would die in a stale cavern at the hands of killers, and the last light that she would ever see would be from some greasy torch.

Why die alone?

An old one posed an age-old question.

They came closer as Demsie wondered. Was it better to take your murderers with you into hell, or leave them to live and hope for God's mercy?

Dammit! None of that even mattered, he was the COD!

Demsie burst from her shadowy crack and squeezed her second plastic bottle, spraying a stream of liquid combustible, marking the both of them. Having no idea what the threat was, they stepped back cautiously several feet.

Then the killers studied her from a safe distance. When one of them recognized her, he laughed. "Shit. It's just Demsie, she's got the chloroform."

That one caught on fire.

When the torch's flame jumped onto his arm, he lurched sideways in shock and bumped into his ally, who Demsie recognized as Frizz.

Frizz looked like a match lighting. He burst into flame and was entirely engulfed in an instant.

He screamed.

The howl had all of the rage and torment that could be expected, for a guy who suddenly found himself deep underground and being bathed in hellfire. He expressed his rage on the killer who had been stupid enough to ignite him in the first place. Frizz punched his associate in the teeth and knocked him flat, and then he turned his attention towards Demsie.

Her body shook, partly from the expectation of her own death at Frizz's hands, and partially due to guilt at what she had done to these two men.

The guilt got the best of her. "Drop and roll! Frizz, drop and roll."

Frizz paused to think. A battle raged behind his eyes. His survival training was at odds with his needs for vengeance. Frizz's smoking hands were extended towards Demsie, knuckles tensed, thirsting only to break her small body in two. Then he screamed and threw himself to the ground. He rolled in the dirt as he snarled like an animal. It must have been horribly painful. Demsie cried as she watched.

Then she noticed the other one, behind Frizz. He seemed to be dead on the ground, lying still like a duck roasting on a grill. A small bonfire was burning from his chest, just big enough to cook a wiener.

The light from the human torches flashed off the walls and roof of the cavern, illuminating the area enough that Demsie could see the details of the ancient metal gate that she had been hiding near. Frizz rolled and thrashed on the ground in an attempt to stifle the flames, but the hungry tongues of fire were only minimally abated.

He will die, Demsie thought, and the idea saddened her.

Right at that moment Frizz must have realized it too and he stopped his rolling. His body had been burned beyond the point of salvage. If he didn't die fast, he would die slow, and both of them knew it. With his own fate irreversibly sealed, Frizz remembered his rage towards Demsie.

She squealed as he came at her, skittering back several steps.

His arms were outstretched with the desire to wrap her in the warmth of an eternal embrace. Demsie recognized his intention to give her a hug that would definitely feel more hot than warm.

As he moved towards her, she knew that Frizz had more than enough speed to catch her, but her brain was electrified with the sole need of finding shelter from the flaming hunter. Demsie scampered to her hiding spot and without even the clarity to think, she clicked a latch on the gate and swung the metallic barrier across the hall.

The gate struck the body of the fallen killer which Demsie had chloroformed moments earlier, leaving the passage unsealed. It meant that she was still vulnerable to her smoldering assailant. Guttural sounds came from from Frizz's throat as he slammed into the bars of the metal gate.

"Ghuaaargh!" He growled as he groped through the bars at her, moving and thinking more like a zombie than a trained killer.

She wondered why Frizz didn't simply go around the barrier as her eyes wandered to the uncomfortably large gap. If Frizz stopped groping uselessly through the bars and were to simply go around —.

Dammit. He had seen her looking.

Frizz pulled back his arm and lurched towards the opening. Demsie knew that she couldn't let him get around the gate so she used the only weapon that she had left.

Through the bars, Demsie sprayed a steady stream of fuel into Frizz's face, aiming mostly for his eyes. The fuel did it's job and Frizz's entire head exploded into flame. He lost his direction and then his balance, and then he seemingly lost his will to fight.

Demsie watched quietly as Frizz died. The old ones were laughing.

In the light of the dying fires, Demsie looked at the carnage. She had done all of this and the thought of it made her sick.

As a cloud of guilt settled itself upon her soul, she wandered over to check the pulse of the first killer that she had neutralized. Dead. Poisoned by chloroform.

Smacks would come soon, and what would she do then? Blunder her way into killing him as well? Not likely.

Demsie wanted to just give up, but she knew that she couldn't. She had to press forward.

Resources. Her training told her to salvage what she could from this site, maybe the killers had weapons that she could use.

She hurried to grab her old tools and the killer's blades. She found a roll of sturdy tape on the killer that she had drugged and poisoned, but nothing else of use.

Using one of the killer's long blades, she prodded at the charred pockets of her barbecued victims. Demsie found nothing intact other than a small set of needle nose pliers that were on Frizz, which she found strange considering where they were. She flung them towards her weapons stash so that they could cool. Then Demsie stood over her pile and wondered what to do with it all.

Tactically, she could think of nothing, so she decided to try an intuitive approach.

The pliers might be useful, and the tape as well. She also kept her plastic bottle although she had no idea what she might use it for. With the survival knife, the wire, the light, and one of the long blades in her hand, it would be all that she could carry.

Demsie tucked what she could into her pockets but was left with no room for the pliers. *I should hide them*, she thought. So she opened them up into an X shape, and put them prongs up, under her long mess of muddy blonde hair, with the handle fitting perfectly onto the back of her neck. Using tape, she fastened the pliers securely under her occipital bone. Then Demsie picked up the long blade and the light and prepared herself to go rescue Alastar.

Which way should she go? Away from Smacks to lure him into an ambush? Or towards him so she could break Alastar out before Smacks realized the threat? Whichever way it was, she wanted badly to leave this ugly place. It stank of death.

She looked again at the carnage once again, and wondered why she had ever come on this insane mission.

Because you are insane. The old ones laughed in her head, and she started to cry.

"There there Demsie, don't cry sweet child." Demsie's eyes rose slowly towards the warm comfort of a man's kind voice. It was Smacks. He was leaning casually against the wall, just beyond the dim light of her small electric torch.

Demsie sniffled. "Smacks." She said, surprised by the surrender that she heard in her own voice.

"It's okay Demsie. It looks to me like you put up a good fight."

"I tried!" Demsie dropped her long blade and her flashlight and collapsed into the dirt.

"You did sweetheart. Come on, I'll take you to Alastar."

Smacks took away her tools, her precious resources. He emptied her pockets and took her tape, her wire, and even her survival knife. She was sorry to see it go.

Then he placed his hand on her shoulder and gently nudged her down the hall.

SIXTEEN

Demsie stepped into the underground chamber and saw Alastar, barely conscious, and his body badly abused. A thin metallic cable bound him to some sort of throne-like chair. His pain was like a piercing scream in her ears and Demsie clutched at her head to shut it out.

Smacks was laughing as Demsie writhed there, on the spot. Still clutching her hands to her ears, she whirled around to face Smacks. "He's suffering! You have no idea the pain that you've caused him."

Smacks' smile slid off of his face. "And for that I am truly sorry. I never wanted this, but I've been forced. Your boyfriend needs to learn to be more forthcoming."

"He's the COD!" Demsie screamed at Smacks.

"So he is, the beloved Alastar Daivi. The Legend. He does have more names than most residents, I'll give him that. But you see, I have a problem. It is a problem that I need his help to fix, but helping isn't in his nature, as you learned yourself when you experienced the hot wet embarrassment, of Charlie pissing in your hair."

Demsie remembered it all right — the shame, the anger, and the pain. Her hand drifted towards her hair self-consciously. It was a dirty mess. Then her finger touched metal.

Demsie shivered, and started to cry. Smacks hadn't taken everything; he had not found her pliers. She still had a weapon. Her finger stroked the metal self-consciously and then pulled away quickly before it was discovered.

A weapon. The problem was that she had weapons before, better weapons. The long blade, her survival knife, hell, even the wire could be used to kill someone easier than tiny needle-nose pliers. The tip would be fairly pointy, but the depth of penetration would be negligible.

She knew what a killer would do in her situation. Smacks' neck would be the best target, but Demsie was no killer. Even the thought of plunging her pliers into Smacks' flesh made her nauseous. She had come to rescue, not to kill.

Rescue. That was it! She knew what she needed to do. So she looked toward Smacks angrily, "You're no better than Charlie." She told him.

Smacks smiled. "Are you serious? I haven't pissed on you yet."

"No, but you will — Do worse to me, I mean." Suddenly she knew for certain that her words were true, and a flash of fear soaked her in sweat from top to bottom.

Smacks said nothing. He just looked at her with what almost seemed like sympathy. Of course as a psychopath, Smacks had no sympathy, but for some reason the killer liked to believe that he was a reluctant villain.

In the time that the Demsie and Smacks looked at each other, an understanding was silently reached. Demsie switched to pleading. "Can I — Can I at least have, a moment before we uh, begin?"

"Of course." Smacks nodded.

"Can I, um, say stuff to Alastar?"

"Go ahead."

She turned to Alastar, his head was flopped sideways like a dead chicken, and his swollen eyes were closed. "Alastar?" She said. There was no response.

Demsie turned to Smacks. "He needs to wake up. I can't talk to him if he's not awake."

"Throw water on him." Smacks gestured towards a canteen and a cup resting on the arm of the throne beside Alastar.

Demsie stepped tentatively towards Alastar's limp body. The high-pitched squeal of Alastar's pain increased with every step closer that Demsie got. She kept her hands pressed to her ears to try to keep out the noise. Of course it didn't work a bit, because the screaming was coming from Alastar's soul.

With one hand she grabbed the canteen and poured some water into a cup.

She didn't throw it at him. Instead, she nudged him gently and placed the cup on his lips for him to drink. His eyes focused on hers. "Anyone else?" He breathed. Demsie nodded her head no. It was a small motion, but she saw how it wounded him. All trace of hope fled from his eyes. "Then we're dead." He said.

"Not yet." Demsie said as she grabbed his hand and kissed him gently on the cheek.

"That's enough, lovebirds." Smacks said and Demsie felt herself being yanked backwards by her hair. Then she was dragged to a spot against the wall right in front of Alastar.

She knew that it was time for the violence to begin. There was nothing that she could do so she retreated into herself and contracted into a little ball

---

It was so hard to focus on her. Too hard to keep his thoughts coherent. When Demsie leaned close to him and kissed his cheek he could smell smoke and mud in her hair.

Why?

Why was she even there? None of it made any sense. He wondered if it was even real.

No! He had to stop that. He knew that it was real.

"Not yet." She told him. They weren't dead yet. Her hand was on his. She had pried open his fingers. Pried them open and pressed — What? Something metal.

Whatever it was, he closed his hand around it to conceal it from Smacks.

Alastar watched as Demsie got dragged towards the wall by her hair. She squealed as her small frame was casually tossed against the cold stone. Demsie's eyes where round with fear as Smacks stepped slowly towards her. Then she crumpled to the floor.

Smacks turned towards Alastar and said, something. What? It didn't matter. Smacks would cause her pain now. All for nothing. All for secrets that Alastar didn't have.

Then he remembered. The metal object. She had given him a thing. Alastar's fingers explored the thing, and realized that it was a tool.

Pliers? He had to reason why.

Why? Why, why, why. Pliers. Why wasn't Demsie screaming? Smacks was busy but Demsie was enduring Smacks' cruel attentions in total silence. Alastar hadn't known that an oracle could do that.

Needle nose! They were needle nose, which meant that they had a part that could cut cable.

Demsie had given him freedom from his bondage. It was a precious gift for which she was now paying. Alastar felt the sharp edge of the wire cutter that was built into the pliers. The sturdy blades were only about three quarters of a centimeter long, but they would be strong.

Alastar thrummed the cable with his thumb. It was tight, but there shouldn't be any recoil when he cut it. There would be noise though, and Demsie wasn't helping with her silence. He watched as Smacks tormented the girl, she should be screaming. Why wasn't she screaming?

Alastar knew why. Demsie had retreated into herself. The pain was in her body but Demsie would be trying her best to be in another place.

Smacks turned to look at Alastar. "You could prevent this. Tell me something true for a change. What could you lose by telling some truth?"

"Why? Why do you need to know?" Alastar breathed.

Smacks smiled. "Some people have given me, certain motivations."

"You're a fool Smacks. You'll regret your part in all this, I promise you."

Smacks laughed. "Somehow I don't feel threatened." Then he turned back to Demsie who was listening intently to their conversation. Her breathing looked labored, and she was definitely splinting her right arm against her side, but she remained silent.

"It doesn't sound like Demsie is all that threatened either, Smacks. Is an oracle getting the best of you?" Alastar said the words knowing full well what the words would produce.

Demsie's eyes flashed wide in surprise, as she signaled the betrayal that she felt from Alastar. Smacks' eyes, on the other hand, narrowed. "You want to hear her scream, Legend?" Alastar said nothing. "It can be arranged."

"No." Demsie said softly as she looked up at Smacks. Whatever you're thinking, no. I'll scream, I promise I'll scream. You don't have to do more."

Smacks paused as though considering the oracle's words. "But the Legend does have a point. You have shown that you can endure a great deal of pain, but perhaps you need to also experience loss. Permanent loss. A finger? A hand?"

"No. Please no." Demsie's thin voice was barely a squeak.

Smacks reached out to her and put his hand gently on her chin. "Of course not, child. I would never take from you something so —," He sighed. "So useful. I will take something purely aesthetic. Something as useless and redundant as the oracles themselves."

Smacks hand slid down to Demsie's chest. "If you had tits I would take one, but you're as flat-chested as your boyfriend." He moved his hand back up to her face. Demsie tried to pull away but Smacks' hand locked around the throat with the speed of a viper and the strength of a vice. Her head was pinned against the stone wall behind her.

Alastar readied his pliers, placing them in position to cut the cable that bound him, even as Smacks stroked Demsie's face.

"Such a pretty girl. So pretty, it would be a shame to lose your beauty wouldn't it? I know what I am speaking of, oracle. Just like you, I have grown up with nothing that is truly my own. I've had nothing that couldn't be taken from me in an instant by another person, if they happened to be in the power position. There was nothing to make me autonomous, to make me *myself*, so to speak. Nothing that is, other than my own unique face.

"My eyes, my nose, the shape of my chin and my cheeks. All mine. Even my expression, and my *demeanor* if you will, they are mine to command. No others. And like you, I treasure them, because like you I have hopes that someday I will be free of the Station. And on that day, I had always wished to take my handsome features with me."

Smacks laughed. "I know, I know, it sounds frivolous doesn't it, but I think that you understand a little, don't you?"

"P-p-please. Please Smacks, I'll scream." Demsie screamed. It was shrill and wild and full of terror.

In that moment, Alastar squeezed the tool in his hand. He felt the metallic wire compress, but it didn't break.

Smacks was laughing. "That was a nice scream Demsie, but that was merely a scream that was *for* me, as opposed to *because* of me. Unsatisfying. And you did just hear that your boyfriend called my virility into question, didn't you?"

"It's not what he meant." Demsie's wide eyes pleaded with Smacks. It was useless. She might as well have been pleading with a cold-blooded reptile. She tried screaming again. Louder this time, ending in a crescendo of sobs. Alastar saw that Demsie's eyes were soaked in tears but by the time the noise ceased, he still he hadn't managed to cut the wire.

"I have an idea. Lets play eeny-meanie-minie-mean." Smacks said as Alastar readjusted the pliers again, wondering if they would even do the job.

"Eeny-meanie-minie-mean. Chop a part and make her scream. If she hollers, the cut will be clean. Eenie-meanie-minie-scream." Smacks hand was bouncing around the structures on Demsie's face. Her lips, her eyes, her nose, her cheeks. By the time Smacks' chant was completed, his hand had landed on her right eye."

"No. Please no!" Smacks raised his knife to her eye and Demsie screamed again. Alastar squeezed the pliers with every bit of strength left in his soul, and this time he felt the cord give way.

Smacks' knife point stayed poised a half inch from Demsie's eye as Alastar wrestled to free his hand from the cable. The Legend watched as Smacks' knife drew closer to Demsie's eye. Suddenly his right hand pulled free. As quickly as he could, he transferred the pliers to his other hand and then returned to his original position.

It turned out to be just in time too, because without warning, Smacks lowered his knife and turned to look at Alastar. "I just remembered," He said. "I promised our young oracle that I wouldn't take anything useful. And what could be more useful than an eye." He turned back to Demsie. "I'm very sorry, my dear. All of that terror was uncalled for."

Demsie was shaking from fear. Her teeth chattered together in a staccato rhythm.

"Of course if your boyfriend would come clean, this need not happen at all." Smacks paused and looked back at Alastar. Alastar said nothing. "Very well. Eeny-meanie-minie-mean —."

Demsie was screaming already, and Alastar was gripping the pliers as hard as he could in his left hand. Once again the cord gave way. It cut clean through on the first try, and Alastar pulled the cables aside.

He lurched to his feet and felt the room spin, momentarily. Smacks back was to him, just twelve feet away, his hands still tapping Demsie's terrified features as she wailed.

"Chop a part and make her scream —."

In an instant, Alastar reviewed his options. He could stab Smacks in the throat with the pliers, but if he missed the artery or if Smacks defended, then Alastar would certainly be a quick victim of the bigger man's capable knife. There had to be a more certain way.

"If she hollers —"

The cable! Alastar turned and measured out a three-foot piece of cable and once again set his pliers to work.

"Eenie-meanie-minie-scream." Smacks was done, and his hand was settled onto Demsie's ear.

"Poor child. Poor, poor child. You will look hideous without that pretty little ear, won't you?"

Alastar glanced at Demsie's face. She was beyond terror as Smacks raised the knife to her ear. The girl no longer needed any encouragement to scream.

Alastar finally felt the cable cut through. He wrapped the ends of the wire around his hands as Smacks began carving into Demsie's ear. Blood sprayed as she tried to push the knife away with her hands.

"Hold still child, if you want the cut to be clean." Smacks told her.

Then the big man couldn't speak.

Alastar had the wire securely wrapped around Smacks' throat, crossed in the back for maximum constriction. He himself was latched onto Smacks' back, with his heels hooked low onto the front of the much bigger man's hips. "The knife, Demsie! Control the knife!"

She did.

Even as Smacks lurched to his feet with Alastar stuck to his back, Demsie threw herself onto Smacks' arm, hugging the arm and the blade to her chest, and weighing down the killer's knife hand while Alastar increased the tension on the man's throat.

Eight second's. Whether they would live or die would be decided within eight seconds, the time that a man can stay conscious without fresh blood reaching the key parts of his brain.

Smacks beat on Demsie violently with his left fist, but the girl didn't let go. Alastar was surprised, and impressed. Demsie was definitely more than she seemed. Then Smacks raised Demsie up above his head in an incredible demonstration of strength. Arm, girl, knife and all, and he smashed her down into the ground with an impact that exploded the air out of Demsie's lungs.

Still Demsie held on though. Alastar leaned back and squeezed Smacks' throat, then he felt something give way inside of the large killer's larynx.

He should have been feeling disoriented by know.

Smacks raised up Demsie again with his powerful arm, and then lowered his arm quickly to smash her once more into the granite floor. This time, instead of dropping his weight into Demsie to increase the impact, Smacks loosened his grip on his blade, and whipped Demsie off of his limb with the ease of someone flicking off water. It did not spare Demsie hitting the ground hard.

One thing was certain, it would now be Alastar's turn to take punishment. In his drugged state, it was all something of a blur. Smacks ran him repeatedly into the hard walls but couldn't get Alastar to loosen his grip on the choke cord. Alastar was thinking that he might win, right up until

Smacks ran Alastar into the stone chair.

Alastar felt his head strike hard into the unforgiving back of the chair, and the world blinked dark for a moment. The next thing Alastar knew, he was face to face with a purple skinned version of Smacks. How had that happened?

Alastar squeezed the wire garrote that was still wrapped around Smacks' throat, although had to adjust the angle of pull to suit this new position. Meanwhile Smacks was pawing at Alastar's face and throat, trying desperately to get a hold of something vital while Alastar dodged the bigger man's hands. That was when Smacks changed his strategy and stopped reaching for Alastar's face. Instead, he hugged Alastar's body close to his own. Alastar could do nothing to stop the man. Pretty soon, Smacks had clawed his way up Alastar's body, working upward. By that point he had grasped Alastar's head on either side, with the two meat slabs that Smacks thought of as hands.

Why wasn't Smacks unconscious by then? Eight seconds had gone by already. Then Alastar realized that Smacks must have gotten some blood into his brain when Alastar had blacked out.

Alastar braced himself for what he knew was coming. One. Two. Three head butts. Crushing blows which Alastar could not defend well at all. Each one rocked Alastar's already broken body, and each one loosened Alastar's grip on the wire. Alastar heard Smacks gurgle with a strained vocalization that told him that the occlusion that he had on Smacks' throat was less than perfect.

One more ringing head butt to Alastar's forehead. Bam! It sounded like a shotgun going off. Alastar wondered if his skull had just been fractured. Then suddenly Smacks' eyes rolled and he fell limp to the floor.

Confused, Alastar wondered why. Why was he standing over Smacks' unconscious body? The garrote hadn't been working. Then he looked over at Demsie. She was gone. But where did Demsie go?

"Alastar! Alastar, lets go!"

He turned and saw her. She had blood streaming from her nose, her mouth, and especially from her ear, which hung from her head like a limp flop of flesh. In her hand was the knife that had done that to her, the knife that he now realized had also been Smacks' undoing. Blood was dripping down its blade.

"Let's go!" Demsie grabbed his hand and began pulling Alastar into the darkness of the cavern, fear gripping her voice. "Let's get out."

Alastar grabbed a flashlight off of the floor where it, and other things, had been scattered during the skirmish. Then together, leaning on each other for support, the two children shambled through the network of caves.

When they emerged, it was dark. Alastar suggested that they wait by the entrance until morning rather than risk injury by travelling at night. After all, they were both in terrible shape, but Demsie insisted that they should run.

"Demsie, it's okay, we won. You killed him."

Her eyes flashed big. "But I didn't! I'm not a killer."

"You did Demsie. Remember the knife? You stabbed him."

"No! I didn't, I only hit him with the handle. I knocked him out!"

Then it was Alastar's eyes that flared big. "You're telling me that he's alive! Smacks is alive?" It was more than Alastar could believe. Demsie nodded sheepishly, obviously feeling her ally's disapproval. "Studor's balls Demsie! Help me push this stone back over the entrance."

The two of them willed their broken bodies to shove the granite lid back into place over the hole. Then they replaced the tarp, and piled rocks and dirt onto the entrance. Luckily, rocks were plentiful in that area. After the stones were all in place, Alastar insisted that they stack fallen logs onto the stones as well, just to make certain that Smacks would never again be leaving his tomb.

"I'm not a killer." Demsie said to Alastar as they leaned on each other for support, assessing their work.

Yeah," Alastar knew what she was saying. "But you're not — *not a killer,* either."

Then Demsie began to sob and it was up to Alastar to lead her to a safe place where they could shelter for the night. His little ally seemed so sad to him. So he made sure to choose a place where they could see the stars.

SEVENTEEN

Smacks showed up two days later. He was muddy and smug, with stories of falling into an underground cavern when some earth gave way. He told everyone that he searched for a day before finding a small tunnel, too small for him but better than nothing. He told his fascinated audience that he dug his way into the tunnel and it took him a full day to emerge, into a remarkably deep coyote den.

He told the whole story while laughing.

His allies greeted him with slaps on the back and smiles. None of them even mentioned the bruised and torn up mess that was Smacks' neck, which looked suspiciously like it had been garroted. Nor did they point out the scratchy hiss that had become Smacks' voice, because his larynx had been partially, yet permanently deranged.

None mentioned it but Alastar, and he only in private when him and Smacks drifted off together behind a barracks.

"I told you that you were making a mistake Smacks." Alastar told the bigger man.

Smacks did not have his usual firm, but measured retort. No silky smooth, gentlemanly response to make his opinion clear. He simply glared, eyes cold as death.

Alastar watched him for a while without further comment. "Those eyes will get you killed, Smacks."

Eventually, Smacks pushed some words past his swollen throat. "I'll destroy you Alastar." The words came out as a hiss.

Alastar smiled with as charming a smile as Smacks might have, before his disfigurement. "Don't you mean, I'll destroy you, *Legend*?"

Alastar left him standing behind the barracks, boiling with rage, and unable to even scream.

Of course, Alastar and Demsie's absence from training was grounds for serious discipline. Studor had them apprehended, as soon as they returned to camp. After a visit to the infirmary, they were fed enough to ensure their survival, and then ushered into Studor's office.

Due to Demsie's stricken state, Studor decided that as an oracle, she had been through enough already. Alastar on the other hand was prescribed an extra discipline. He was given refrigeration therapy, to remind him not to miss training sessions in the future. It was decided though, that Alastar would be allowed ten days to heal up from the rigors of the torture that Smacks had inflicted, before he would begin his *therapy*.

While Alastar was shivering in the cold tank, it took him several days to work out in his mind all of the events and decisions, that had left him vulnerable. It took days for Alastar to review the mistakes that had led him into Smacks' clutches. He realized that he had been a fool. A young fool, and he swore that he would not make similar mistakes again.

Since the ordeal, Demsie was clinging even closer to Sophia's side than she ever had before. Her ear, or what was left of her ear, scabbed over and eventually formed into a scar. It could have looked worse. After all, her hair mostly hid the part that didn't heal right.

The experience had changed her though. If such a thing were possible, Alastar believed that Demsie was behaving even crazier than she had before their time underground. He knew that the oracle would adjust though, because she had to. Living in the Station simplified such things.

Alastar knew that he needed to adjust as well. His methods needed an overhaul. From that point on, Alastar and his allies' survival would be dependant on the decisions that he made. If they were going to live past merely being Station residents, Alastar was determined that he would learn to play the *long game*.

In the future, he intended to exercise foresight, and plan his life as though it were a chess match. That would be the smarter way. Unfortunately, he also knew that he had an impulsive nature. Many of his gifts relied on quick tactical decisions and bold gambles. Besides, as a psychopath, what was the point of being fearless if you spent your entire life exercising caution?

Alastar determined that he would laugh more, play harder, and make his enemies pay, one day. He was certain that the right day would present itself at some point in the future. But when that day did come, he would need allies with him. Alastar recognized that now.

There would be a time for revenge. On Smacks, Devant, Bartus, and maybe even Charlie. Until then though, Alastar would wait, and he would grow stronger. Stronger than any of them. Until that day, he would build the Legend.

She knew that she was taking an incredible risk, but her friend Demsie was capable of distracting the Keeper for a few minutes at least. Sophia pushed open the door and slipped inside.

Revulsion swirled in her stomach. It was chilly, and her boy was strung up like a side of beef.

Sophia went to him in quick steps and wrapped her body around him, pressing tight so that she could give him some of her heat.

It was no use. Anger flashed inside her heart. Her boy was barely conscious.

She had known that it would be just like that. Sophia pulled the thermos out of her bag. Unscrewing the cap, she poured some of the warm liquid into Alastar's mouth.

"I love you." She told him.

Acknowledgements

As you might assume, I've had some help in getting this book to print. I can only give my sincerest thanks to everyone who has offered advice or support. Aside from my family, pretty much all of the people who have given me guidance have been patients of mine—so because of that, I will acknowledge you privately. You know who you are though.

Thank you. Truly, thank you.

FREE DOWNLOAD

If you haven't already, sign up for Braedan's Reader's Group and get a compelling story guaranteed to transport you into the world of the Covert Existence — **FREE** of course.

Of course there's **More Covert Existence**!

The battle is not over. Their enemies are not yet vanquished. Their futures are not guaranteed. Live the struggle in **Book Two**

For updates about new releases, as well as exclusive promotions, visit the authors website

www.Braedanlalor.com

Have you checked out the other books in the series?

CLICK BELOW TO GET STARTED

(http://www.amazon.com/author/braedanlalor)

ABOUT THE AUTHOR
Braedanlalor.com

Athlete, fighter, poet, healer.
Always subservient to the story.
Thinker, muser, watcher, truth.
The mysteries are worth the search.
Father, brother, husband, son.
The roles we play to find the higher

It's hard for me to take this part of the book seriously. In my mind I keep hearing Dr. Evil played by Mike Myers, sharing his life's story with his counseling group — "My father was a relentlessly self-improving boulangerie owner from Belgium, with low grade narcolepsy and a penchant for—" You get the picture. Anyways, people tell me that readers might be interested in who I am, and what my not-so-covert existence is like.

By this time in my life I've got some wear on the tires though, and the task is not really that simple. I could talk about my day job (Physical Therapist and trainer of professional and developing athletes, biomechanical sport skills analysis, as well as being a so-so businessman). My passions (Surfing, people, laughter, fun). My family (just think half the Winterfell Stark's, meets Bob and Doug McKenzie). My origins (I've lived in Canada's frozen prairies, subtropical Florida, and moderate Vancouver Canada). My competencies (sports in general, fighting, surviving tough things, writing, and any type of talking, including BS). My incompetencies (fixing and building, singing, conforming, walking away from conflict, author biographies, and answering questions the easy way). Or my pets (Rocco and S'more).

All of that is nice but much of it is notably unimportant though. It's trivia and I need to view it as secondary interests to storytelling and the quest for truth. You may have guessed that those are the topics that for some reason I feel free to exposit on —in long meandering diatribes fueled by gin soaked tears, while typing my finger bloody (Yes, I am a one finger typer — but I've written over fifteen books as well as some academic works like that, so don't you hate).

Go to my website if you want to find out what drives my storytelling, (or to find out how to develop your own typing finger to the relative strength of a third century Shaolin monk.)

http://www.Braedanlalor.com

If you like my Writing

There's a way that you can help me.

Reviews — Are. Huge.

With just a few keystrokes, in your own words, you can tell other readers that these books are worth looking into. By doing so you can help me get views on Amazon, fund my writing, and get all fifteen of my books out to the public before I go utterly and completely mad.
Which is a real possibility.

Instructions:

1. With Amazon account active, click the link in step 2.
2. This is the link to my Author page so you can find the book
3. Go to the specific book's page (by clicking on the cover) and then scroll down
4. On the book page click the yellowish "**Write a Customer Review**" button

Have fun typing what you like!

Printed in Great Britain
by Amazon

26864660R00088